DATE			

Big Money

by the same author

DEEP AND CRISP AND EVEN
DEAD KNOCK
FAIR FRIDAY

PETER TURNBULL

Big Money

ST. MARTIN'S PRESS
NEW YORK

Library of Congress Cataloging in Publication Data

Turnbull, Peter.
Big money.

I. Title.
PR6070.U68B5 1984 823'.914 84-11791
ISBN 0-312-07846-3

First published in Great Britain by William Collins Sons & Co. Ltd.

First U.S. Edition

10 9 8 7 6 5 4 3 2 1

CHAPTER 1

Thursday, October 10

That particular Thursday was a bitch: a real bitch. The wind came from the north-east, the rain was cold and hard and the sky, when the dawn came, would be grey and low. The first bad weather of the winter had come suddenly to the city of Glasgow and Myra O'Shea had woken up to it, suddenly. She lay in bed listening to the rapid tick of the clock, to the wheezing of her still slumbering man, a wheezing which seemed to touch deeper and deeper recesses of his chest, and she listened to the rain hammering on the roof of their old tenement. She was awake before the alarm went off and when it did ring, loudly jangling nerves, she clambered out of bed and dressed hurriedly. Before she left her flat she laid the breakfast table for her man. She set out the bread and the butter and put teabags in the teapot and made sure the kettle was full. He had a hard job and she didn't feel right unless she left him something to help him start his day. She stepped out into the close as quietly as she could and started down the stair which wound round the square walls of the close, and a leak, the same one as last winter, let rainwater drip from the roof down four floors to the ground floor where it splattered on the flagstones in the close mouth. Myra O'Shea stepped into the street. A torrent was running in the gutter. There was a milk float driven by a milkman swathed in sweaters and a plastic mackintosh. A bus drove by, empty and with all the lights on. Otherwise the long street was deserted. She turned and walked up the hill and the rain ran down her face. It was 6.00 a.m.

Myra O'Shea reached her place of work, the Post Office

on Maryhill Road, at 6.20 and let herself in the back door. As soon as she turned the second key the burglar alarm sounded, very loud and very shrill. The alarm was connected to the police station and sometimes the duty sergeant would 'phone up just to check that all was OK, especially if Myra O'Shea was delayed in switching it off. Most times they didn't telephone, because at that time in the morning small lights glowed on a panel in the police stations as hundreds of head cleaners moved quickly from the rear entrance to the alarm switch. Myra O'Shea pushed up the alarm switch up with her thumb and two fingers and then ambled back to the door. She picked up her shopping-bag and shut the door, locking it with one of the locks. Having peeled off her coat and plastic head scarf and hung both in the closet so that they dripped into the sink, she went to the kitchen at the back of the building and started spooning tea into a huge teapot. She plugged in the electric kettle and sat down for her first cigarette of the day while she waited for it to boil. For the first half-hour the cleaners sat and smoked and drank tea and blethered. At 7.00 they set to work cleaning and polishing and disinfecting, all except the lazy one who just walked round with an aerosol spray. They each worked an alloted territory and at 8.15 they finished work, brewed up, blethered, went home and returned at 5.00 in the evening.

There was a knock at the back door. Myra O'Shea rose and walked down the corridor. She unlocked the door and stepped aside as a second cleaner, hunched and dripping, entered the building, complaining bitterly about the rain. Myra O'Shea left the second cleaner to shut and lock the door and returned to the kitchen where the kettle was gushing steam and rattling. She found it a very satisfying sight and sound, especially on such a morning when the sky was black and the rain was drumming on the windowpane.

The two cleaners sat at a table drinking tea and smoking. There was an anxious tap on the door and while Myra O'Shea rose and went to answer it, the second cleaner, Robyn by name, poured out a third cup of tea and laid a cigarette beside it. When Myra O'Shea returned to the kitchen she wasn't accompanied by the third cleaner, she was accompanied by a man. He wore a balaclava with a horizontal bar so that only his mouth and eyes were visible. He had a combat jacket, olive green trousers and leather boots which laced high up his shins. In his hands he held a shot-gun which had been sawn off at the barrel and the butt. The man stepped into the room; he was followed by another and another and still another. The four men stood in a semi-circle around the cleaners. They were all dressed in a similar manner, all armed with sawn-off shot-guns. Myra O'Shea sank into her seat, white-faced. She said, 'Oh my!'

The man who entered the room first slid his left hand from the barrel of his shot-gun and held the index finger up to his lips. The two cleaners nodded, understanding and acquiescent. Two other men began pushing tables and chairs to one side of the room, thus clearing a large floor area. The first man signalled the two cleaners to stand and move to the far side of the room. This they did, backing away nervously from the black balaclavas and the firearms. When the two women reached the far wall he motioned them to sit down. The fourth gunman put his shot-gun on the table at which the two cleaners had been sitting and put his hands on his head. The two women did likewise. The first man made a circling motion and the two women swivelled and sat facing the wall with their hands on their heads.

There was a knock on the door. One of the gunmen left the room and returned a moment later, pushing two frightened-looking middle-aged women in front of him. The first man extended his arm and pointed to the other cleaners and the two women joined their colleagues, sitting on the floor, facing the wall with their hands on their heads.

It was 6.35 a.m. They began the long wait. The four women on the floor, the four hooded gunmen standing. Not a word was spoken. For nearly two hours the only sound heard in the room was thc rain on the window and the growing rumble of traffic on Maryhill Road as the bitch city groaned into life. Then at 8.25 a.m. came the first tap on the door as the staff began to arrive, the junior ones knocking for admission, the senior staff unlocking the door with their keys. Two gunmen remained in the room while the other two loped silently down the corridor. They stood behind the door and opened it, letting in a man in his middle twenties who had his collar turned up against the rain and stepped quickly into the building. The door was shut behind him, he turned, smiling, and met the gaze of a man in a black mask, holding a gun. The young man made to shout, but the gunman shook his head and pointed down the corridor as another employee began rapping on the door. The man had joined the cleaners on the floor of the room at the back of the building before the door was opened again, this time to let in two young women who complained bitterly about being kept waiting in the rain, their voices stopping abruptly as they realized the enormity of what was happening. The staff began to arrive rapidly, in ones and twos, some knocking on the door, the more senior turning a key in the lock. All were quickly and efficiently shepherded into the small room at the back of the building. One or two more were heard running through the rain towards the door, which was opened for them before they knocked; in such cases the employee would step into the corridor panting thanks only to be shocked into silence by the sight of a man with a gun and a balaclava which showed only his mouth and eyes.

At 8.36 one of the gunmen began counting the heads of the people who sat on the floor. He counted twice and then nodded to first gunman. All four gunmen then relaxed and began a second wait.

On the floor Myra O'Shea began to whimper. A young woman told herself she should have realized something was wrong when the door took a long time to be opened. A middle-aged undermanager tried to figure out what the four men were going to do, then felt his heart sink into his stomach as he realized that it was Thursday morning. One young male employee gradually and he hoped imperceptibly began to inch his head around. Eventually he looked into the barrels of a shot-gun and turned quickly back to face the wall. The man next him wished the gunmen would speak, even harsh threats would help ease the tension. But they didn't speak, not even to each other, they just stood there, occasionally pointing their guns at someone who moved too much. He, too, had realized it was Thursday and he wondered if he could issue a warning? He wondered what would happen if he forced their hand; would they shoot if he made a rolling tackle to the nearest one? Would he get support from the others? All it would need would be for one of the women to scream or one of the guys to heave something through a window. But what if the guns were loaded? What if these guys were as cold-blooded as they were efficient? A shot-gun blast at this range would blow someone in half. He decided it wasn't worth it, not even for a quarter of a million smackers it wasn't worth it. That and his three-month-old daughter made it no contest.

It was a long dragging three-quarters of an hour until 9.15 when the sound of a diesel engine was heard at the rear of the building. There was a crunch of gears and a squeal of brakes as a large vehicle manoeuvred in the yard. The gunmen became agitated and Myra O'Shea could feel the tension rising. There was a sharp knock on the back door. Three of the gunmen left the room and went down the corridor. The door was heard to open, there was a shout, the diesel engine started up and stopped again, there was the sound of a scuffle, a man groaned loudly, more shouts, a squeal of brakes. Seconds later a man shouted 'OK' and the fourth gunman left the room.

Andy Scott who had wondered about the possible success of a rolling tackle was the first to get up. His legs were cramped and stiff and they were weak with fear, but he made it down the corridor and to the back door in time to see a red estate car lurch out of the yard and disappear from view. At his feet, lying half on and half off the step was one of the security guards. He had blood on his face and was holding his stomach. He looked up at Andy Scott and tried to say something. Scott staggered back down the corridor to the back room, but when he got there somebody else was already on the 'phone. So Scott said, 'Red estate car.'

'They're in a red estate car,' said the man on the 'phone.

'Yes, four men.'

'Six,' said Scott.

'No,' said the man, 'there were six, two others must have been outside. 'My name? Middleton. I'm the manager.' Outside it was getting light and the rain had stopped.

PCs Phil Hamilton and John Piper were on traffic patrol. They received the Code Two at 9.18. Hamilton reached forward and grabbed the microphone. He pressed the 'send' button and said, 'Charlie Delta Foxtrot, responding,' as Piper switched on the blue flashing light and the klaxon and began to force a path through the rush-hour traffic. On their radio they heard other area cars: 'Tango Delta Foxtrot, responding,' 'Charlie Mike India, on our way.'

Charlie Delta Foxtrot was the first car to arrive at the Post Office. Piper swung the car into the driveway at the side of the building and turned into the yard. The two cops saw an armoured van with its doors open, one security guard lying on the ground being tended by his mate and a young woman. Piper left the car and ran towards the building while Hamilton snatched the microphone, pressed the 'send' button and said, 'Charlie Delta Foxtrot—confirm raid on Post Office, at least one casualty. Ambulance requested.'

'Ambulance already dispatched. Out.' The female voice crackled in the static.

Hamilton replaced the receiver. Before he left the car he heard control broadcast: 'All mobiles, continue to keep sharp look out for red for Roger estate car, six occupants, believed armed and dangerous. Observe and report. Do not attempt to apprehend. Control out.' As Hamilton left the car, Tango Delta Foxtrot screeched into the yard with lights flashing and klaxon sounding. It was closely followed by Charlie Mike India, the driver of which had switched off his klaxon and also, Hamilton noted, had arrived on the scene and pulled up just as smartly as Tango Delta Foxtrot, but with much less show.

The six cops on the scene were all constables, but it was Piper, a sergeant bursting out of his constable's uniform, who took command.

'Phil,' he said, addressing the slower moving Hamilton, 'do what you can for this guy.' He indicated the wounded guard. Then, raising his voice: 'Will you move the cars against the far wall, the ambulance will have to get in. One of you get to the top of the driveway, make sure it doesn't get blocked.' He went inside.

One or two people were milling about the corridor looking dazed or excited, but most employees were still in the room where they had spent the last hour, or, in the case of the cleaners, the last three, sitting on the floor. Chairs had been pulled from the mound of furniture and placed in the centre of the room. Some employees, mainly the middle-aged, sat on them, but two young women also sat on chairs, their heads bent towards their knees. Many were talking, few were listening. When Piper entered the room there was a second's silence. Someone said, 'Thank God,' and then people started talking at him.

'Four of them.'

'They had guns.'

'And masks.'

'Didn't say anything.'

'Hurt a security man. Did you see him outside?'

'They were here when we got to work.'

'OK, OK.' Piper held up his hands. 'We'll be taking statements from everybody in due course. Meanwhile we'd like you to wait here. Is anybody hurt? No, right, anybody in shock?'

'These two ladies fainted,' said a woman who was resting her hand on the shoulder of one of the young women who sat with their heads bowed.

'Did they hurt themselves as they fell?' asked Piper.

'No, we caught them.' It was a young man who was pulling furiously on a cigarette.

'Right,' said Piper, 'so there's no one for the ambulance.'

The ambulance at that moment pulled up at the side of the armoured security van. One or two people who were standing in the corridor walked to the door. Piper stepped into the corridor and said, 'Will you come and stand in here, please?'

Detective-Sergeant Ray Sussock was the first CID Officer

to arrive on the scene. He turned the battered unmarked Police Department heap into the narrow lane beside the Post Office and met the ambulance coming the other way. Sussock reversed into the street and when the ambulance had gone, he drove once again into the lane and pulled up in the yard. He was met by Piper.

'Armed raid on a security van, sir,' said Piper. 'One man, a security guard, injured. Nobody else hurt. Raiders apparently waited in the Post Office for the van to arrive. Opened the back door of the Post Office when the security guard knocked on it and clobbered him. There seems to have been four inside and two more on the outside. Red getaway car. Couldn't get the registration number.'

'Yes, I heard the alert,' grunted Sussock. 'How much did they get away with? Do you know?'

'I heard the figure of a quarter of a million pounds mentioned, sir,' said Piper.

Sussock whistled. 'Not a bad rate of pay for a few seconds' work,' he said. 'Beats police rates. We'll have to get all the staff including the security firm personnel to P Division where we'll take statements. There are two minibuses following me. I anticipated that we'd need them.' He smiled a self-congratulatory smile. 'With them, my car and the three area cars I see here that should be sufficient transport.'

'Very good, sir,' said Piper, 'I'll ask the employees to make their way into the yard.' He returned to the room and as he entered it he heard Middleton on the 'phone.

'Yes, sir . . . yes, sir . . . The entire consignment . . . I believe so . . . I haven't yet had time to check . . . the police are here already . . . It was the first thing we did, ring the . . . No, sir, but one of the security men was injured . . . Well, bad enough to need an ambulance . . . Yes, sir, I'll do that, as full as possible . . . Thank you, sir, goodbye.' Middleton slammed the 'phone down and turned to Piper. 'The attitude of the man,' he said. 'My God, you'd think I had a part in it.'

'Did you?' asked Piper.

'That, Officer' snarled Middleton, 'is not funny.'

'You're telling me,' said Piper. Turning to the larger assembly, he raised his voice and said, 'Can I have your attention, please? We're going to take you to the Police Station which is at Charing Cross, near the city centre. You probably know the building. We won't be detaining you long, we will be taking a statement from each of you and then you will be free to leave. So now will you please make your way into the yard and await the transport which is on its way. Please do not touch anything as you leave the building.'

Middleton said testily, 'I have to write a notice and stick it on the main door.'

'Please carry on,' said Piper.

In the yard Sussock stood by the door. He had been pacing up and down the yard, but the cold air of the first winter weather was beginning to hurt his chest. It was, he knew, a legacy of being a heavy smoker in his twenties, more than thirty years earlier, and he knew that if this wet cold bitch of a morning was an indication of the winter ahead, then he was in for a hard time until April. April! Oh, God, it seemed an age away.

'But it's starting to rain again.' The woman waited as she stepped into the yard. Her friend behind her said, 'Why can't we wait inside?'

'Because we don't want to disturb the interior of the building,' Sussock said patiently, 'certainly not any more than we have to. Your transport will be here any minute, in fact . . .'

Two white minibuses, each with the orange flash of the Strathclyde Police, swept into the yard.

'Just climb aboard, please, ladies and gentlemen,' said Sussock, walking to the first minibus and opening the side door. He turned to the driver. 'Back to P Division, as quick as you can.' The young driver nodded.

Hamish Middleton had found a dry marker and wrote on a sheet of paper 'Closed due to unforeseen circumstances' and added directions to the next nearest Post Office. When he had finished he turned to Piper. 'I'll have to go and put this in the window by the front door.'

'Very well,' said Piper. 'Don't touch anything.'

'They didn't penetrate the building,' Middleton protested.

'I'll wait here,' said Piper.

Piper, walking behind Middleton, was the last out of the building. 'Seat in the car for you, sir,' said Piper. He indicated an area car which stood in the yard, with one of the rear doors open and the engine running. It was Charlie Delta Foxtrot with Phil Hamilton at the wheel. Piper walked with Middleton towards the car and as Middleton slid on to the rear seat and pulled the door shut, Piper opened the boot and took out his yellow cape. He watched the car leave the yard, slipped on his cape and walked back to the rear door of the Post Office. He stood there. He was alone in the yeard. There was the security van, still with the doors open, and at his feet the drizzle washed a pool of blood into the drains. It was five minutes before 10.00 a.m.

The Post Office employees and the driver of the armoured security van were taken to the elderly building which housed P Division Police Station. The Police Station was built in 1926 and had rapidly become cramped and overcrowded, with the situation aggravated by staff being evicted from rooms so that up-to-date police technology, such as computer terminals and radio transmission equipment could be housed. There were seats in the reception area by the front desk for half a dozen of the Post Office employees. The rest had to stand. One by one they were asked to step into one of three interview rooms where statements were being taken.

In one of the rooms PC Phil Hamilton was taking statements. He was twenty-four years old and a plodding, methodical cop. His father had worked for John Brown's shipyard and had had a working man's respect for education. He had taught his son a rhyme by Rudyard Kipling:

> I keep six honest serving men,
> They taught me all I know,
> Their names are What and Why and When
> And How and Where and Who.

The rhyme had remained fresh in the mind of the growing Hamilton and he wrote the six interrogatives in the front of each new notebook and used them to help him question suspects, mentally ticking off each one as it was answered. On this particular day he had written What, Why, When, Where, How, Who on a piece of scrap paper which he placed at the side of the paper on which he was to write the statements.

The door of the interview room opened and WPC Willems, tall, blonde, strikingly good-looking even in the unflattering serge uniform, showed Myra O'Shea into the interview room.

'Please take a seat,' said Hamilton as WPC Willems shut the door behind her. He looked at Myra O'Shea, who seemed to him to be very nervous and still very unsettled and then he looked at the six words at his side. He took Myra O'Shea's name and address and said, 'Well, Mrs O'Shea, if you'd like to tell me in your own words what happened this morning I'll then ask you points I'm not clear on.'

'Yes, sir,' said Myra O'Shea to the man who was young enough to be her grandson. 'Well, I woke up early and got up when the alarm went at six. I heard the rain and put out an extra round of bread for my man because he needs food in the bad weather . . .'

Hamilton listened patiently, writing down that which he thought relevant.

In the next room a man in an ill-fitting uniform was gesticulating wildly as he spoke.

'Wouldn't have got in, not in a million years, not with they pop-guns,' he said. 'Our van can withstand shot-gun blasts, we've seen tests and the company has a rule, if anybody comes up to the van with a shot-gun don't open the door 'cos he can't get at you. Just start the motor and drive off. So I heard a scuffle and saw these guys in combat gear, masks and sawn-offs, so I pressed the starter motor. Then a car, red Ford estate it was, reverses down the drive and this guy gets out, dressed like the others only he doesn't have a sawn-off, he's got a high-powered rifle and he points it at my head. Well, I was in the army, I know how powerful rifles like that are. This guy, he can have what he wants so I open up. He drags me out and I go over to where Timmy is. Another guy yells OK and other guys came tumbling out of the Post Office and start separating the van from the money. They form a chain and chuck the bags from one to the other and pile it in the estate car. They left the bags with the mince.'

'Mince?'

'Coins, change. They just took the paper money. Lighter and more valuable, I reckon.'

'Did you get the number of the estate car?'

'No, kept it side on. I was more concerned for my mate anyway. Can't say I was really bothered about number plates and such.'

In the third room Andrew Scott said, 'The thing that got

me was the silence. They were cool, calm and collected. They never spoke, not even to each other. They seemed to know exactly what they were doing, seemed to trust each other. Really professional.'

'That right?' said the cop who was taking the statement. He underlined that observation.

'Yeah,' said young Scott, and added, in a manner which suggested he was an aficionado of gangster movies, 'They knew how to handle artillery.'

'What do you mean?'

'Well, like I said, they were calm and gave simple and clear instructions and then only once. I mean, when they told us to keep quiet they did so by putting their fingers to their lips, they didn't wave the guns about like cowboys, they didn't threaten to blow our heads off like neds would have done. When they wanted us to sit they pointed at the floor, they never actually threatened us with the guns, if you see what I mean. They held them and everybody saw them, but they didn't prod with them or point with them. That made the guns more frightening, somehow. Like they didn't have to prove they could use them.' Again the cop underlined what he had written in the witness statement.

Detective-Inspector Fabian Donoghue turned his Rover into the driveway which led to the yard at the back of the Post Office. He parked his car behind two other vehicles, walked past the armoured van and entered the Post Office. Piper saluted him as he passed.

Inside the building the Scene of Crime Officer was positioning his camera on its tripod preparatory to photographing the floor. Donoghue stood by him, looking at him silently. The Scene of Crime Officer, unused to the Inspector's way of requesting information, was slow on the uptake. Then: 'Oh, I see, good footprint in the dust, sir,' he said. 'Lucky they didn't come in after the cleaners had washed the floor.'

'Indeed. Carry on.' Donoghue stepped carefully past the area of the floor which was squared off with white chalk marks. In the back room Donoghue found Jimmy Bothwell. He was a forensic assistant, he had moved to the Police Department from his post as chemistry assistant in a secondary school. He had mannerisms and a lack of confidence which suggested a man who was much younger than his thirty-six years. Donoghue stood in the doorway and looked at Bothwell.

'Not a lot, sir,' said Bothwell awkwardly, 'er . . . quite a few fingerprints, sir, but I think most must belong to the folk who work here.' He blinked at the Inspector from behind his thick-lensed spectacles. 'I'll record them all, though, just on the off-chance that . . .'

'I should think so,' said Donoghue.

'The only definitely promising thing I found was this, sir.' Bothwell held up a self-sealing Cellophane sachet. Donoghue had trouble seeing anything in the sachet at first, but then noticed a small strand of green fibre lying in a fold at the bottom. 'It was stuck here, sir.' Bothwell tapped a doorcatch on the frame of the doorway which led to the small kitchen.

'Good, good,' said Donoghue. 'So far that's our only clue. That and a red car. Get it processed as soon as you can.'

11.35 a.m. Detective-Constable Matthew 'Ding-Dong' Bell turned his unmarked car into a quiet street of tall tenements at the back of Maryhill, near the Botanical Gardens. Ahead of him, half on and half off the kerb, was a red Ford estate with one of its rear passenger doors still open. Bell slowed his car to a stop beside the Ford. He looked inside. The keys were still in the ignition, the hand-brake was not applied. Bell returned to his car and sat in the driver's seat as a sudden squall turned the drizzle into hard-driving rain. He listened to the rain hammering on the roof of his car and then took the microphone in his hand, pressed the 'send' button and said 'Tango Zulu Foxtrot to control . . .'

Bell waited with the getaway car until back-up arrived. A Scene of Crime Officer bolted a second steering-wheel over the first so that the car could be driven without damaging any latents which might have been left on the steering-wheel. The big Ford lurched off the kerb as the driver fought with the unfamiliar clutch. The car was driven into the city and to a large covered area at the rear of the Department of Forensic Science. The moisture on the body of the car was evaporated by two large hot-air-blowing fans and when the metal was dry, aluminium powder was spread over the surface and then gently dusted with fine brushes to reveal any fingerprints which might have been left. The car's registration number was fed into the Police National Computer. Moments later the printout was handed from one officer to a second; it gave details of a white Ford estate stolen in Carlisle two days previously.

'Quick respray and a dash up the A74,' said one officer.

'Helps us, that,' said the other. 'I mean, any prints on the surface of the car are going to belong to our boys; the owner's prints will have been painted over.'

'Yes,' said the first drily.

The forensic chemists worked slowly and carefully, sweeping the aluminium powder across the roof and bonnet of the car with gentle strokes of a slim brush. The filings would adhere to the impression left by a thumb or finger and the print would be outlined and then photographed.

Detective-Constables King and Montgomerie watched the chemists work from the corner of the covered area and were dismayed to see the camera bulb flash only three times in the course of the sweep of the bodywork.

And that, to their particular dismay, included the area around the doorhandle and the bonnet catch. An hour and a half after they started to inch their way over the surface of the car, the chemists turned their attention to the interior. One took the front and the other the rear, where the seat had been folded down to give a flat carrying capacity. The two chemists each took a wad of self-sealing Cellophane sachets and, using a pair of tweezers or cotton wool, collected small items, hairs, bits of grit, a smear of grease, a strand of fibre, before beginning to dust for prints.

Montgomerie and King stood patiently. They knew they were in for a long wait.

'Fancy nipping round the corner for a pint?' suggested Montgomerie. 'It *is* lunch-time.' He was tall, broad of chest, with a flat stomach. Angular features and a neat down-turned moustache.

'Better not, my son,' said King, smaller, bearded, chubbier, 'better not.'

When the forensic chemists had finished lifting samples and had begun to brush the interior for latents, a Scene of Crime Officer approached King and Montgomerie. He smiled as he drew close and raised a six inch by ten inch manilla envelope to chest height.

'Hot off the press,' he said. 'One very good print, we're running that through the computer right now. Plus two photographs showing that one of the gang had a tear in the tip of the one finger of one glove. Not bad, eh?'

'Oh, terrific,' said Montgomerie, taking the envelope from the enthusiastic Scene of Crime Officer. Enthusiasm was better to meet in one's colleagues than lethargy or perfunctoriness, but even enthusiasm drained one at times.

'Is that all you can come up with after two hours?' King raised his eyebrows.

'Well, that's only the outside, chief,' said the Scene of

Crime Officer, 'and it took diligence and patience to get that. The inside of the car should be more forthcoming.'

'You reckon?' said Montgomerie.

'Sure to be. But don't build up your hopes, boys, these guys were professionals.'

'You don't have to tell us,' said King. 'Twenty-six hours in the day today.'

Montgomerie's stomach began to rumble.

'Don't remember me, do you, son?' said Hamish Middleton in the interview room. 'My wife's disappearance,' he persisted, with a smile.

Hamilton looked at Middleton. 'Sir?'

'You were at the desk when I came in to report my wife's disappearance. You don't recall. Well, it was a good two years ago, right enough.'

Hamilton confessed he did not recall opening a missing person's file in respect of a Mrs Middleton. He swung the completed statement round. 'Please sign here, sir,' he said.

CHAPTER 2

Donoghue leaned back in the chair behind his desk. He was wearing a dark blue three-piece suit with a gold hunter's chain looped across the front of the waistcoat. He pulled on his pipe, a modest bowl with a slightly curved stem. He smoked a special mix which was made up for him by a tobacconist in George Square, a Dutch base with a twist of dark shag for depth of flavour and a slower burning rate. He was reading the witness statements which had been taken that morning. He read each statement three times, pulling thoughtfully on his pipe as he did so and, by 4.00 p.m. his office was full of a light blue haze which hung in layers and had a stronger smell than its colour might indicate.

He put the last of the witness statements down and walked to the window of his office and stood looking out across the sunken motorway and up Sauchiehall Street. It was early rush hour, the pavements were beginning to fill, the cars and buses nosed bumper to bumper out of the city towards the suburbs. It occurred to Donoghue that many Glaswegians would, at that moment, be reading the *Evening Times*, a copy of which lay on the hard chair next to his filing cabinet. He had had it brought up with his mid-afternoon coffee and, having read it, had laid it upside down so that he did not have to look at the headline: ARMED GANG GRAB £¼M FROM CITY POST OFFICE.

He turned from the window and resumed his seat, drumming his fingers on the witness statements, all of which gave a clear picture of what had happened, though none could give an indication of who had perpetrated the raid. Nothing was said by the raiders, except the one who had shouted 'OK', and none of the witnesses had been able to identify anything about the voice from that small utterance. There was not one physical characteristic which was apparent in respect of any of the raiders: none was very tall, or very short, or very fat, or very thin, none had a peculiar gait. They were all 'average', 'average', 'sort of average'. The word had been used so often in the statements that it had become meaningless.

Donoghue inclined his head and looked up at the fluorescent bulb shimmering behind its perspex cover. He began to trawl his mind for the positive information contained in the statements: six men, who were able to carry out an obviously well planned robbery without speaking, who each knew exactly what to do, and who could remain calm in the final stages when the armoured van was pulling up outside the building and the hostages had been contained for over two hours. They were professionals and that kind of league isn't reached without accumulating some form on the way. It was, therefore, highly likely that the names and fingerprints and photographs of all six raiders were somewhere among the banks of information stored in the Police National Computer. But Donoghue knew that if he asked the collator for information on all known British felons with convictions for robbery and violence, aged between twenty-five and fifty-five, who weighed between ten and fifteen stone, stood 5ft 8ins to 5ft 10ins tall and were currently at liberty, then he would receive a printout at least eight inches thick and crammed with names. He also knew what a dispiriting task it could be for a cop to knock up felons and write down alibis in notebooks, to say nothing of it being an utter waste of man hours. He knew he had to narrow down the field: he needed to be able to home in on something.

There was a tap on his door. Donoghue sat forward and picked up the first statement on the pile. Then he said, 'Come in.'

Richard King came in and closed the door. He carried two manilla envelopes; one large, one smaller.

'From Forensic, sir,' he said, approaching Donoghue's desk and handing him the envelopes. Donoghue put the witness statement down and took the envelopes from King. The larger envelope contained a number of black and white photographs. There was also a letter from the Scene of Crime Officer offering a commentary on the photographs. One print showed the rear of the Post Office, another the armoured van, a third showed the footprint in the hallway, 'rubber-soled boot, size 8, wearing evenly,' read the commentary. There was also a print which showed what a security guard with a broken jaw looks like. Half a dozen prints showed the getaway car from half a dozen different angles. From the prints he could tell that the car was a Ford estate with a rear seat folded flat. He could tell very little else. Donoghue selected a print and handed it to King.

'Get hold of the negative of that print and have it duplicated in poster form to be put up in libraries, bus and rail stations,' he said, 'with a caption like "Did you see this car in Maryhill on October 10th?" and so on, I'll leave the details to you. We're conferencing the raid in Chief Superintendent Findlater's room tomorrow at nine a.m. We've got precious little to go on so we had better have some action to report by means of compensation.'

King took the print from Donoghue, 'Who'll be at the conference, Sir?'

'The Chief Superintendent and my team including you. Day off tomorrow, wasn't it? Still owe you Christmas Day from last year, don't we?'

'Yes, sir,' said King.

'Well, cancel it and come in.'

'Will that be all, sir?'

'Is Montgomerie in?'

'He's in the canteen, sir. Having a coffee before he goes off duty.'

Donoghue snatched the 'phone on his desk and dialled a two-figure internal number. 'Montgomerie there?' he said. 'Ask him to come to my room, please, tell him he can finish his coffee first.' Donoghue replaced the receiver.

'He was on duty at 6.00 a.m., sir,' said King.

'I know that,' replied Donoghue quickly. 'But as I keep saying, if he, and you for that matter, wanted to punch a time card you shouldn't have joined the Police Force. Not in this city anyway.'

King grunted. His two children were still very young, too young to miss him much, still needing their mother before they needed him. It was his wife he felt sorry for, he must seem to her to be more like a lodger, a stranger who comes in for his supper and falls asleep on his bed still half clothed, too tired even to wash, and who wakes in the morning to find that someone has covered him with a blanket. He gets a mug of tea brought to him each morning and all about him are half-finished jobs, the door stripped of its paint eighteen months ago and still not repainted, the cupboard without its doors, the shelves still lying in the spare room. Rosemary, a Quaker, moved silently but purposefully about their home, she wore her hair in a bun, was so good with the children, and never, never, complained.

'What,' demanded Donoghue suddenly, 'is that?'

'It's a photograph of a mark left by the glove with a tear at the tip of one finger, sir,' replied King in a matter-of-fact manner. 'It's the only thing we seem to know about the raiders, that one had a torn glove.'

'That, and the fact that they were sort of average,' said Donoghue wearily.

'There were a couple of good ones of the same fingerprint,' said King, 'but I took them out.'

'You did what?'

'They belonged to DC Bell. We ran it through the computer.'

'He found the car?'

'That's right, there was another print inside.'

'Bell's too?' said Donoghue testily.

'Yes, sir.'

'I'm surprised at Bell, all that experience, glowing references from the Lothian and Borders Police, and he goes and leaves his dabs all over the getaway car. He's a clown.'

'There was just the two, sir. Nothing else was disturbed.'

'Even so. Well, don't stand there, get on with that poster.'

King left Donoghue's office and a few moments later

Montgomerie knocked and entered. Donoghue guessed that the two officers had met in the corridor and had stopped to exchange a few words, most probably starting with a warning from King. There was, Donoghue noted, a look of weary resignation in Montgomerie's eyes.

'I know you were supposed to get off at two, Montgomerie,' began Donoghue, looking down at the surface of his desk before he looked up at Montgomerie. 'I also know it's now after four, but we have to move on this robbery, we've not turned up any leads and we're conferencing it tomorrow at nine o'clock sharp. Make a note of that.'

'Yes, sir.'

'We haven't any leads, and so I'm anxious to show some action to the Chief Superintendent. King is having posters of the getaway car run up. I'd like you to organize a reconstruction.'

'Of the robbery?'

'I think of just a red Ford estate driving from the Post Office to where it was found on Garrioch Road would be sufficient, Montgomerie. Have it run through the streets at about eight-thirty tomorrow. You'll need six masked men inside the car and officers on the street at intervals along the route. You'll need to enlist the co-operation of the Uniform Branch and I want you to represent the CID. I'll accept the reconstruction as an excuse for your late arrival at the conference. Shouldn't take you more than a couple of hours to organize. Then you can sign off.'

'That's very kind of you, sir.' Montgomerie's voice had a slight trace of sarcasm.

'There was an incident in the summer, Montgomerie,' said Donoghue coldly, once again looking down at the grey steel top of his desk. 'One man died as a direct result of your indiscretion. You were placed on a probationary period and your performance will be reviewed in eight months' time. You would do well to remember that.'

Montgomerie remained silent.

'Who's in the building? CID, I mean?'

'Just Abernethy, sir.'

'In the CID rooms?' Donoghue grabbed his telephone.

'Yes.'

'Where's Bell?'

'Signed off duty, sir.'

'He didn't hang about, did he?' Donoghue growled as he again dialled a two-figure internal number. 'Abernethy, DI Donoghue, step into my office, will you, please?' He replaced the receiver and glanced up at the young and good-looking detective-constable who stood in front of his desk. 'Well, Montgomerie, the sooner you start the sooner you finish.'

'Where do I get a red Ford estate car, sir? We don't have any in the car pool.'

'Use your initiative, man. Haven't you any contacts in the motor trade? Most coppers have. Didn't you put business in the way of a garage whenever you attended a motor accident? Strictly against regulations, but it got you a bottle of whisky at Hogmanay and a packet of cigars from time to time, didn't it?'

'Well, since . . .'

'Right, get on with it and don't even dream about hiring a car. That would give the chief apoplexy. There's financial cuts elsewhere and I haven't yet told him we've overspent this month's budget and we're only ten days in. You can't run a service without paying for it, but just try telling that to the wise men. All right, man, get on with it.'

Montgomerie turned sharply and left Donoghue's office. Alone again, Donoghue tore open the second envelope that King had delivered to him. It was the report from the Forensic Science Department. Before he could read it there was a knock on his door.

'Come in.' Donoghue slipped the report into the envelope and placed it on his desk as Abernethy entered the room. By comparison to other officers, he was short and lithe. He was in fact shorter by a full inch than the minimum five foot eight inches required of all recruits, but was nevertheless let in to the Force by a shrewd recruiting team who recognized initiative and leadership potential behind Abernethy's wide-eyed nervousness.

'Take a seat.' Donoghue waved his hand towards the chair in front of his desk. Abernethy sat dutifully, perching slightly forward.

'Don't tell me you expect to get off soon too,' said Donoghue.

'Not until ten o'clock, sir,' replied a bewildered Abernethy.

'That makes a change,' said Donoghue, half to himself. 'I have a little job which should keep you busy until then. You know where the getaway car was found, on Garrioch Road?'

'Yes, sir.'

'Good. Now, young Abernethy, I want you to walk from one end of Garrioch Road to the other, walking up each stair and calling at each flat. There are houses only on one side of Garrioch Road, the other side is the Botanical Gardens, so there shouldn't be more than two hundred flats. Take a note of any flat from which you don't get an answer and call back tomorrow. At approximately nine-thirty this morning, the tenth of October, six men, probably still wearing hoods but certainly still dressed in paramilitary fashion, halted their red estate car and transferred themselves, their goods and chattels, including five firearms and a quarter of a million pounds, into a second vehicle. On one side of the road, as I have said, is a public gardens where people exercise their dogs and through which they walk on their way to work. On the other side of the road is a long line of four-storey tenements with bay windows. There would have been a sudden flurry of activity at about nine-thirty this morning and I am disappointed that the public-spirited people of the district have not already come forward, because I refuse to believe that nobody saw anything. So off you go, Abernethy, and if you can't come back with at least three good witness statements, then don't come back at all.'

Abernethy nodded and stood and walked quickly out of Donoghue's office. As soon as Abernethy had left his office, Donoghue snatched his 'phone again. This time he dialled 9 for an external line. When he heard the solid 'click' and then the soft purr of the dialling tone, he dialled an Edinburgh number. 'Hello, it's me . . . I'm sorry, I'm going to be late . . . Of course I can't help it, damn it. It's near the end of the week, do you think I want . . . I am not shouting . . . I know I promised him, but you'll have to take him. . . . How? How can I if I'm not going to be there? I'll take him to South Queensferry on Sunday, we'll go crabbing, he likes that . . . it isn't unreasonable . . . I'm not ill-tempered . . . look, just expect me when you see me.' And then he hung up.

Flicking his gold-plated cigarette lighter rapidly, he managed with great clumsiness to light the blackened tobacco in the bowl of his pipe. The smoke was bitter but he still pulled strongly. He took the Forensic Science Department report from the envelope and tried to read it, but he found he could not take anything in. He put the report down and took the pipe from his mouth. She was right, of course. Early forties are dangerous years for a man pushing hard in his career, blood pressure problems, heart disease, why, there was this guy only thirty-seven and he keeled over one . . . No, it's not worth it, just not worth it. Calm down. Calm down. So he put on his overcoat and his trilby, signed himself out and strolled to the river and back.

It was dusk. The rain had moderated to a slight but persistent drizzle. The air was cool and refreshing and Donoghue breathed deeply as he walked. The stroll relaxed him, he was able to put the robbery into perspective, his thoughts were clearer but, as he re-entered P Division Police Station and signed in at the front desk, he could not rid himself of a nagging anxiety that he would have little progress to report at the conference.

Back at his desk with his pulse a steady eighty beats per minute, he excavated the charred tobacco from his pipe and treated himself to a fresh plug. He lit it calmly and carefully, playing the flame from his lighter over the bowl. When it was drawing smoothly he settled back in his chair and read the report submitted by the Department of Forensic Science.

Forensic Science Dept,
Strathclyde Police,
G3.

October 10th

Detective-Inspector Donoghue,
P Division,
Charing Cross,
Glasgow.

Ref: Robbery—Maryhill Post Office—October 10th.
Report on the forensic examination of the Scene of Crime and of the motor vehicle understood to have been used as 'getaway' vehicle.

A thorough sweep of the scene of crime has revealed

little information. I have forwarded a copy of the photograph of a footprint which was apparently left by one of the raiders. As I explained to the two CID Officers who attended the Forensic Science Department, the footprint was apparently made by a rubber-soled boot, to fit foot size eight.

A strand of fibre was located in a door lock. This was examined and proved to be similar in weave and dye to the material used in garments known as combat jackets.

An examination of the car proved to be more rewarding. There were a considerable number of latent fingerprints in the vehicle, number thirty-five in all. Of these, thirty-three appear to belong to the same person and are clustered around the driver's seat. We append copies of two other fingerprints found in the car. Print B was found inside the glove compartment where it had been lodged in a film of grease. This print may be some months old. Print C was located on the inside panelling of the rear of the car at a point which is only accessible when the rear seat is folded down to provide a flat carrying space. This print is also thought to be quite dated. All prints have been submitted to the Police National Computer with the request that any information forthcoming be transmitted to yourself.

In the rear of the car we found fibres belonging to a heavy sacking of the type believed to be used in industrial operations, a cluster of blades of grass identified as marram (*Ammophilia arenaria*).

The car itself appears to have been involved in an accident. There is a sound but untidy welding on the front nearside wheel arch and suspension mounting. The car body in that area has been beaten out. This indicates that the car sustained damage to the front near side.

I hope this information is of use.

J. Kay,
M.Sc., Ph.D.

Donoghue took a manilla folder from his desk and in black felt tip he wrote on the cover, 'Post Office Raid 10/10'. It would do until the clerical staff provided a proper file with a case number and a front sheet. Inside the folder he placed the witness statements and the photographs and report from the Forensic Science Department. He drummed his fingers on the cover and then lifted the telephone once again. He dialled another two-figure internal number.

'Collator?' he said. 'DI Donoghue here. I'd like all you can tell me about a car, with particular reference to previous owners and previous accidents. Thank you.'

'About everything?'

'Sorry?' said Abernethy.

'Everything,' said the man, calmly.

Abernethy thought that the reason why the man had not reported to the Police could be explained by the fact that he seemed to be at least eighty years old and walked with an aluminium walking stick in each hand. But his hearing was good, his thought process seemed lucid. Abernethy hoped only that his eyesight had held up equally well. He had started to knock on doors at 5.00 p.m. and it was now 7.30 and this old guy was the first to have admitted seeing anything. The folk who lived alongside the 'tannies', as they called the Botanical Gardens, were not obstructive, they were polite, concerned, curious and helpful. But they had not seen anything of the raiders dumping the getaway car. Except the old chap. Abernethy glanced at the plastic nameplate screwed on to the door. 'Perhaps you could tell me what you saw, Mr McGeechie?'

'Here? Or would you care to come in, son?' Mr McGeechie turned slowly and began to walk down the hallway of his home. He had shiny white craggy hands which gripped the handles of his walking sticks. Abernethy stepped into the hallway and shut the front door behind him. Mr McGeechie had a room and kitchen. Abernethy, following the slow-moving, elderly man, had ample time to glance in to the kitchen. There was a black cast-iron range set in the wall and a pulley hanging from the ceiling. In the sitting-room there was a bed in the recess and two chairs round an old open fire. They were deep and heavy armchairs covered in leather similar to ones Abernethy had noticed in the waiting-room of his dentist. One armchair was piled high with cushions. There were solid storm shutters on the windows, and the whole flat seemed, to Abernethy's untrained eye, to be completely original, unlike all others he had visited in Garrioch Road, which had over the years been gutted and modernized. Mr McGeechie stood in front of the chair which had been filled with cushions and then turned through one hundred and eighty degrees and finally sank into the cushions, his arms and the walking sticks vibrating as he did so. He transferred both walking sticks into his right hand and laid them against the side of the chair.

'How long have you lived here?' asked Abernethy, sitting in the second chair.

'All my days, son.' He raised his arm and pointed. 'On that bed I was born, and on that bed I'll die.' McGeechie then indicated a faded black and white photograph which stood on the high mantelpiece. 'That's me in the army, between the wars. I served seven and twelve, seven with the regulars, twelve in the reserves. I was in the Cameronians, the Glasgow Regiment, served in Turkey, Egypt and India.'

'Any active service?'

'No. I was a peacetime soldier. Still, the army was rough between the wars. I remember it well.'

'Remember this morning well?' asked Abernethy, smiling.

'Aye. There's nothing wrong with my memory or my eyes. It's my body that's failing me. Arthritis in my arms, legs and spine. Once I could wrestle three men, now . . .' The man held out his hands towards Abernethy. The skin was shiny in some places, dull in others, mottled on the backs, with hard gnarled nails on the ends of quivering fingers. 'Old age is a curse, son,' said McGeechie. 'I'll be glad when I'm done.'

'You don't mean that.'

'Aye, I'm no good. I've had more than my three score and ten, I've been around long enough.'

'This morning,' Abernethy prompted.

'The to-do in the street, you mean?'

'That's it.'

'Men with guns?'

'Yes, can you tell me what you saw?'

'I was at the window, taking the air. I got up with the daybreak. Rising early in the summer, long lays in the winter. The gardens are just across the street. I take an interest in the seasons and I like to watch the changes. This morning I was up with the first light and I got to the window twenty minutes later. I saw this car come tearing round the corner and it slowed down as it drove along our street and it stopped more natural like, right under my window.'

'Under the window? This window here?' Abernethy turned and looked at the bay window.

'Yes. Across the road from the tall larch tree. See the leaves we can see out of my window?'

'Yes. Where the bird is?'

'Yes. Those are the top branches of the larch tree. The

car stopped right opposite it.'

Abernethy turned to face McGeechie.

'Well,' continued the old man, 'they scrambled out of the back of the car, four of them. Two got out of the front.'

'Masks?'

'No. Army gear but no masks. They looked like soldiers, I don't mean how they were dressed, but the way they did things, ye ken? Doing things without thinking, without being ordered to, like they had done it a hundred times and at the double. Efficient, sergeant would have been pleased. Formed a line and tossed about fifteen or twenty bags from the car into the van and drove off, calm as you please. About two hours later I saw a young man come by and stop and look at the car. I thought he must be a policeman in plain clothes, so I stopped watching then.'

'You stood at the window for two hours?'

'On and off. I kept going back to my chair for a wee rest when my legs got tired.'

'You said the men had guns?'

'One rifle and some stubby guns. Nothing I've handled, son, but I seen them on TV. Sawn-off shot-guns.'

'Now,' said Abernethy, 'this is quite important, Mr McGeechie. You said that these men didn't have masks. Could you describe any of them?'

'One. I didn't like what I saw so I picked one out and concentrated on him, you know. There were six of them, but I could only describe one.'

'Good enough.'

'Aye, well. He was a man, that's obvious. Now he had black hair.'

Abernethy scribbled on his pad.

'He was stocky, a bit like my first sergeant, may he roast in hell, may he dance round the fire, he was about five and a half feet tall, broad in the chest, he'd make a good quarter-back, sort of pitched his body forward as he ran. I noticed that. I played for the company.'

'The company?'

'D Company, Cameronians.'

'I see.'

'In my young days. I was young once.'

'Age?'

'Eighty-one.'

'No, I mean the guy in the street.'

'Oh, about thirty-five, seven.' The old man coughed. 'He looked a hard wee guy.'

'Hard?'

'A fighter. Hard eyes. Grim face.'

'Clean-shaven?'

'Could've done with a shave. Wouldn't pass muster. Can't say he had a beard or a wee 'tache, if you ken?'

'Aye. Weight?'

'Ten/twelve stones.'

'A wee thug in fact,' said Abernethy.

'Aye,' nodded McGeechie. 'You could say that. A wee thug.'

'All right,' said Donoghue, 'stick with it and I'll try and get this out on the nine o'clock bulletins and it will certainly be in the morning papers. How long do you think it will take you to do the rest of the street? . . . Couple of hours? . . . I see, well, I'll wait here until nine-thirty and I'll call it a day if I haven't heard from you by then . . . Oh, Abernethy, this is a good piece of work.' Donoghue replaced the telephone receiver and immediately picked it up again and dialled 9 for an outside line and then a local number. When his call was answered he said, 'DI Donoghue here, P Division CID, we'd like your help in publicizing information in connection with the raid on the Post Office in Maryhill this morning.'

'Fine,' said a cheery voice down the 'phone. It sounded young and enthusiastic and Donoghue thought that he had not heard it before. 'We'd like a code word.'

'Oh damn,' said Donoghue.

'Procedure as laid down by your own Executive. I could dig out the memo reference for you.'

'You needn't bother,' said Donoghue. He had wedged the 'phone between his shoulder and head and was using his hands to hold and turn the key of a metal box which he had taken from his desk drawer. He took a book from the box and ran his fingers along a line of words. 'Today is October the tenth.'

'Right.'

'Code for the day is "Sound of Sanda". What is it this time, geography of Scotland?'

'Not entirely, we're working our way up the west coast. That will keep us going for a couple of months. We don't know what we'll use after we get to Cape Wrath, but as we're still down on the Mull of Kintyre we've got a bit of time yet. If we don't think of anything, I dare say we'll just carry on round the top and down the other side. We might even make it very exotic by taking in the Orkneys and the Shetlands. Anyway Sound of Sanda is wrong. I'll have to assume you're some bampot who wants us to announce that the Red menace is advancing on the Rhine, good—'

'Wait!' snapped Donoghue. 'It's been a long day.'

'Certainly has,' said the voice. 'Sound of Sanda was *last* Thursday. What does it say underneath the Sound of Sanda?'

'Isle of Gigha,' sighed Donoghue, shutting the book.

'What can we do for you?'

'Do you have a pen and notebook ready, I don't want to repeat myself.'

'No need,' said the voice, the chirpiness of which was beginning to irritate Donoghue. 'This is being recorded.'

'I might have known,' Donoghue groaned. 'OK, male, thirty-five to forty, probably looks older, clean-shaven but may have a few days' growth, dark hair, short, stocky, about five eight and ten to twelve stones, wearing army-type clothing. That is a description of a man the Police wish to interview in connection with the Post Office raid in Maryhill this morning. Will you add that he's armed and dangerous and the public are asked not to approach this man, but to contact the nearest Police Station.'

The voice broke in: 'Both radio stations, both TV stations, morning papers, tomorrow evening's paper. How's that grab you, daddy-oh?'

'I find the prospect most pleasing,' replied Donoghue drily as he replaced the receiver.

At 11.00 p.m. the tall man turned the key in the lock and stepped into the hallway. The rush of warm centrally heated air served to make him feel even more tired but he managed to shut the door quickly behind him to prevent too much heat escaping into the night. The woman approached him and stood on her toes and kissed him.

'They tried to wait up,' she said, taking the man's hat and briefcase. 'But they didn't manage to stay awake.' The man grunted and shook his coat off his shoulders.

'Your meal's in the oven,' said the woman, folding the coat across her arm.

'Uh.'

'Too tired?' she said. 'Coffee, tea, cocoa?'

'Cocoa.'

'I'll bring it in the room for you.' She hung the coat up in the wardrobe which stood in the hall and then went into the kitchen to prepare the hot drink. But by the time she brought the steaming mug of cocoa into the sitting-room Fabian Donoghue had fallen asleep in the armchair.

*

In a house in Cambuslang the young man looked into the old man's room.

'What time is it?' rasped the old man from his bed.

'Just at the back of eleven, Dad.'

'What's the weather?'

'Clearing up, Dad.'

'Just in from your work?'

'Aye, Dad.'

'What time is it, son?'

'Just at the back of eleven, Dad.'

'Weather still wet?'

'No, it's beginning to clear, Dad.'

'What time is it?'

'Eleven, just gone, Dad.'

'Hard day?'

'Hard enough.'

'Well, good night, son.'

'Good night, Dad,' said Abernethy.

In the old damp house the man crushed another empty lager can and tossed it on to the heap of trash by the fire, which they only lit at night. He looked across at the other men and smiled. One of the other men grinned and said, 'They haven't a clue, chum, believe me. Don't know what hit 'em.'

CHAPTER 3

Friday, October 11

WPC Elka Willems carried three tables, one by one, from adjoining rooms and stood them end to end in the small room at the opposite end of the CID corridor to DI Donoghue's office. She placed seven chairs against the tables and laid a pencil and notepad on the table in front of each chair. She collected the 'in conference' sign from the front desk and returned to the CID corridor and hung the sign on the door, but left the door wide open so as to avoid confusion. The conference was scheduled for 9.00 a.m.; it was now 8.59. She smiled to herself; all in order with sixty seconds to spare.

She was sitting on the chair at the bottom of the table, near the door, when the lumbering bulk of Chief Inspector Findlater entered the room. Elka Willems stood. Findlater walked down the side of the room and sat in the chair at the head of the table. He moved slowly, deliberately, as indeed it was said he had built his career: a slow, deliberate plod from the quiet streets of Elgin and a constable's uniform to the rank of Chief Superintendent in Glasgow, all within an honourable thirty years. Donoghue followed Findlater into the room and sat at the Chief Superintendent's right hand. Detective-Constable Richard King, bearded and a little overweight, sat, modestly, as near to the bottom of the table as he could. Abernethy, slender and nervous in his movements, sat opposite him. Detective-Sergeant Raymond Sussock, tall, greying, stumbled as he entered the room and sat opposite Donoghue on the left of Findlater. Detective-Constable Bell was last to enter the room. He was tall and well built with a striking head of red hair. He grinned as he sat next to Ray Sussock.

'One seat still vacant,' said Findlater, nodding at the gap between Donoghue and Richard King.

'Montgomerie,' said Donoghue. 'He's attending a reconstruction of the incident, sir. I gave him permission to be absent from the conference for that purpose. He'll be along as soon as he can.'

'Very good.' Findlater nodded to Elka Willems who stood and shut the door. She returned to her seat, took up her notebook and ballpoint and scribbled at the top of the page: 'Minutes, Conference 11/10.'

'Well,' began Findlater, 'can we formally convene

the conference about the armed raid at the General Post Office in Maryhill which took place at approximately eight-thirty yesterday morning, the tenth of October.' He paused before continuing. 'We will first review and assimilate all intelligence. We then receive feedback on action and progress so far. Then we will address ourselves to action.'

Elka Willems scribbled on her pad.

'So, Fabian, I wonder if you would be kind enough to summarize events for us?'

'Certainly, sir.' Donoghue leaned forward. He took his pipe from his jacket pocket and cradled it in his hands as he spoke. 'The raiders first entered the Post Office by a simple subterfuge. They let the first cleaner unlock the door and switch off the alarm. The second cleaner arrived and was let in by the first. The raiders then knocked on the door themselves and the cleaners already inside the building opened the door, assuming the knock to be one of the other cleaner's. The raiders then quite simply took control of the inside of the building and, as the staff arrived, they were directed into a room at the back of the Post Office and made to sit on the floor with their hands on their heads. It was a Thursday, when most of the weekly counter payments are made to the unemployed people in the manor. Consequently delivery of a large consignment of cash was made that morning, as indeed it is made every Thursday morning, and as usual it came in an armoured truck operated by the usual security company. As soon as the truck pulled to a stop, a fifth raider pointed a high-powered rifle at the driver, who did the sensible thing and surrendered and opened up the van. At this point three of the four raiders still inside the Post Office came out and started to transfer the paper money—they left the bags of coins—into the estate car which in the interim had pulled up behind the security van. Also at this point there seems to have been a scuffle between one of the security men and a raider and the security man was knocked about a bit, a fractured jaw and, we later discovered, a ruptured spleen . . .'

'Condition?'

'Stable. In no danger.'

Findlater's sudden question had interrupted Donoghue's flow and he searched for words before he could pick up the thread again. 'Yes . . . oh yes, the raiders made their getaway, they numbered six in all, one was always at the wheel of their getaway car which was later found in Garrioch Road. I think I'll ask DC Abernethy to continue on the basis of a witness statement he took yesterday evening.'

Abernethy fidgeted on his chair. Elka Willems, sitting only inches away from him, could feel his nervousness. 'Sir, yes, sir. I was calling on all flats in Garrioch Road, well, only one chap saw anything, amazing really . . .'

'You get used to that,' growled Findlater. 'I get the impression that half the public walk around with their eyes shut, don't you agree, Fabian?'

'Well . . .' said Donoghue. Then he turned to Abernethy and said, 'Carry on, son. Take your time.'

'The transfer was observed by an old gentleman who lives on the top floor just above where the getaway car was found. He seems to have seen the incident, that is the abandoning of the car. The raiders moved the cash from the estate car to a delivery van and drove off quite sedately, apparently. He was able to give a good description of one of the raiders, which was circulated.'

'Yes. I saw the paper this morning.' Findlater leaned back on his chair. 'What were your feelings about this man as a witness?'

'Well, sir, he was elderly but he seemed sharp enough, mentally I mean, he also seemed to have good eyesight. Might not exactly be twenty-twenty vision, but it was good enough to make out what was happening. His account seemed reasonable, it wasn't hazy, yet it didn't have the excess of details which might indicate good imagination rather than good eyesight. In terms of him as a court-room witness, giving evidence and all that . . .' Abernethy shook his head. 'We couldn't use him in my opinion, sir—er—respectfully, I mean. He's over eighty, he can hardly walk, he was pleased to talk to me, but I don't know how he'd cope under cross-examination.'

'Well, at least it's a lead,' said Findlater. 'Anything else?'

'Forensic came up with a couple of things,' replied Donoghue. He opened a folder which he had brought into the conference and handed Findlater a copy of the report from the Forensic Department.

'Couldn't keep your hands to yourself, could you, Bell?'

'Sir?' And then Bell smiled.

'All over the bloody getaway car, inside, outside, everywhere, your prints were.'

'Only two or three I heard, sir.' Bell relaxed his smile a little, but he was still smiling. Donoghue didn't like the way Bell seemed to be sailing close to the wind and he sensed anger rising in Findlater and saw the Chief Superintendent's huge hands tighten their grip on the sheet of paper.

'One or two other prints have been lifted, sir,' said Donoghue, hoping to ease the tension he felt rising in the confines of the small room. 'They have been fed into the computer, but we haven't any feedback yet. They also found some Marram grass on the rear of the estate car and evidence of surgery on the front wing.'

'Surgery?'

'I'm using the word lightly, sir.' Donoghue smiled, but not in the deliberately provoking manner employed by DC Bell. 'It's been welded up and hammered back into shape.'

'Is that relevant?'

'Probably not, sir. I'm merely reporting the findings of the forensic team.' Donoghue put his pipe between his teeth and drew on it before continuing. 'Fibres from the raiders' combat jackets have been found, but I'm afraid that tells us little since we already know from eyewitness accounts what they were wearing. One footprint was also found on the floor of the corridor. Many others had been trampled, but one distinct impression of the sole of a size eight boot survived intact.'

'So we're still . . .'

There was a knock at the door. Elka Willems left her seat and opened the door to reveal Montgomerie standing on the threshold.

'I'm sorry I'm late, sir . . .' he began as he entered the room.

'Inspector Donoghue has already explained,' said Findlater. 'Sit down.' Montgomerie took the one vacant chair between Donoghue and King as Elka Willems shut the door. 'Any response from the recreation?'

'None when I left, sir.' Montgomerie shuffled in his seat. 'But you can never tell with things like this, we might have succeeded in jogging someone's memory, but the reaction might be delayed. One of the Panda cars and the station wagon we borrowed will remain at the location where the getaway car was found for another hour or two before calling it a day.'

'Very good.' Findlater began to make notes on the pad of paper in front of him. 'Does that conclude the feedback?'

The meeting was silent.

'Very well.' Findlater suddenly seemed unsure of himself. 'You seem to have come just in time, Montgomerie, we're going to start discussing action and apportioning the work. Right then, where do we go from here . . . er, Fabian?' Spoken, thought Montgomerie, like a man who's chairing a meeting and hasn't a clue where to go from here. He reminded Montgomerie of a maths teacher at Montgomerie's school who plainly did not understand mathematics and who would spin out the lesson as long as possible by talking about motor-cars and cracking jokes, by spending as long as he could writing a trigonometry problem on the blackboard, and then go and sit on the desk of the ablest boy in the class and say, 'Right, Robert, how do you think we should tackle this?'

Donoghue lit his pipe and seemed to Montgomerie to be making a point of taking his time over it. 'Well, sir,' he said, laying his gold-plated lighter on the table, 'I would suggest, with respect, that we start by attempting to match the description we have of one of the raiders with known criminals, a plough through the mug-shots in fact. If we can identify him he may well lead us on to the others, because it seems that this is a pretty slick outfit and may well have operated together before, and each may well have accumulated a bit of previous.'

Findlater nodded.

'I would also suggest that we follow up the firearms lead. Sawn-offs are ten a penny, but a high-powered rifle, that's something else entirely. Someone, somewhere must have reported such a gun being stolen. That may well prove to be an interesting scent to sniff. The money, unfortunately, wasn't in sequenced numbers. Customers in High Street banks get the new notes, the unemployed get the old notes, but it's still a large amount of money, even if it is divided six ways. It will have to be laundered somehow, so any unusually large deposit in banks or building societies should be brought to our attention. So should anyone attempting to buy a car with a suitcase full of used pound notes. A few telephone calls should alert the right people. There's still feedback to come on the two latents found in the car, sir.'

'Very well,' said Findlater, leaning forward on the table. 'What do we have for action? Minute these, please.

Searching through records for known villains who fit the one description we have. Follow up any high-powered rifles reported stolen or missing during the last—'

'Twenty-four months,' said Donoghue without raising his head.

'Two years,' continued Findlater. 'Phone round the banks and the big car dealers and the like. Ask them to let us know if anyone has been throwing money around. Any other points?'

Silence.

'Inspector Donoghue will coördinate the operation.'

'Thank you, sir,' said Donoghue.

'Will you give me a daily report, say at four p.m. each day?'

'Certainly, sir.' Donoghue pulled on his pipe.

Findlater stood and left the room. The others too stood and filed out one by one. Eventually only Detective-Sergeant Sussock and WPC Elka Willems were left in the room.

'About three o'clock this afternoon?' said Elka Willems. Sussock patted the notes he had made during the conference. He shook his head. 'Who can tell when I'll get off?'

She smiled. 'Just come round when you can,' she said.

Ray Sussock was fifty-four years old and had recently been granted permission to extend his service with the Police Force. That, and his rank of detective-sergeant, in his more melancholy moments, he felt were in recognition of length of service, rather than his ability as a cop. The bright young men who sat at the conference table, he thought, would reach his rank before they were out of their twenties. Donoghue, his immediate superior, was more than ten years his junior. The old man of the Division, to be nursed along, given the easy jobs, the short straw numbers. He replaced the receiver and ran his ballpoint through a telephone number which he had written on his pad. He read the number immediately beneath it and dialled. 'Hello, this is P Division Police Station at Charing Cross, I'd like to speak to the manager, please, . . . thank you . . . Uh, good morning sir, DS Sussock, P Division. I'm telephoning your bank, and other banks in the city, in connection with the raid on the Post Office in Maryhill yesterday . . .'

Donoghue sent the file down to the typing pool with a red sticker demanding priority attention. By 11.00 a.m. it had been returned with all the recordings and reports typed up. At 11.15 Elka Willems showed him the minutes of the conference which she had written out in longhand in her spiky European style of writing. He read them, murmured his approval and signed them. By 12.30 they too had been typed and were included in the file. Donoghue rose from his chair and left his office. He avoided the cramped room on the ground floor of P Division which was optimistically referred to as 'the canteen' and, as usual, went out for lunch. It was shortly after his return, two minutes before 1.30, that the case began to crack. The 'phone on his desk was ringing as he entered his office. He picked it up.

'*Brassica oleracea*,' said the voice on the other end of the line.

'I beg your pardon?' Donoghue loosened his belt: the pizza seemed to be expanding inside him.

'*Brassica oleracea*,' the voice repeated.

'You'll have to excuse my ignorance.' Donoghue walked round the side of his desk and sat in the chair. He was curious as to the identity of the voice, but he didn't force the pace of the conversation. He knew the call would not have been put through to his room without the constable on the switchboard being told who was speaking. There was, however, a noticeable tone of impatience in Donoghue's voice.

'Sea Cabbage,' said the voice, brisk, efficient, female.

'Sea Cabbage?'

'You'll recall we found traces of *Ammophila arenaria* in the getaway car?'

'Oh I see, this is with reference to the raid on Maryhill Post Office.'

'Yes, Dr Kay here from Forensic. I thought I had made that clear.'

'Not very,' said Donoghue. 'Your call was put through to my extension without explanation. I'll see the officer on the switchboard about it.'

'Well, anyway, I don't know whether this is important, or not, it really isn't for me to say, but I felt you ought to know that among the *Ammophila arenaria*, that is the Marram grass which we found in the car, we have just now located a spore of *Brass* . . . Sea Cabbage.'

'I confess,' said Donoghue, 'that I did not know there was such a beast.'

'You may be forgiven for that, Inspector, it is a very rare beast, as you might say. Now I don't want you to think that I am presuming upon your area of responsibility, but I have taken the trouble to ascertain the locations of the known colonies of Sea Cabbage around our shores. They cluster mainly on the south and west caost of England and Wales, but there is also a small colony on the Mull of Kintyre.'

'There is?'

'It's the only one in Scotland, a bit of an anomaly in distribution pattern apparently, being at least a hundred and fifty miles further north than any other known colony. I dare say the Gulf Stream wafting along the west coast helps it to survive. If there's a thriving tropical gardens in Ayrshire and palm trees on Rothesay front, I can't see why botanists get so excited that a predominantly English and Welsh plant should be found flourishing in Scotland.'

'Yes, I can think of another exotic plant which seems to be flourishing in the West of Scotland, judging by the number of reports we're submitting to the Procurator Fiscal.'

'What?' said Dr Kay.

'Nothing,' replied Donoghue. 'You were saying, Doctor?'

'What's that? Oh yes, well, Sea Cabbage flowers in August and the spore we have seems to be about two years old.'

'So the car was in the vicinity of the Sea Cabbage colony on the Mull of Kintyre about two years ago last August.'

'Probably.'

'Uhm,' said Donoghue.

'Well, there might not be any relevance to it, that's for you to decide.'

'I certainly appreciate your thoroughness, Dr Kay. Where abouts on the Mull is the colony of Sea Cabbage?'

'Near Machrihanish.'

'Right down at the bottom?'

'Yes. Now the other point of interest is that we have identified one of the two latent prints we found in the car.'

'You have? Excellent!'

'The computer gave us a "no trace" printout on one, but the other belongs to one Flora Middleton. The case is held . . .'

'The case?' said Donoghue. 'She has a record?'

'Only as a missing person,' said the scientist. 'Beyond that I know nothing. All that is your department.'

'Yes, I'm sorry I interrupted. The case is held by?'

'Yourself, Mr Donoghue. That is, your Division.'

'Thank you, thank you very much, Dr Kay, thank you indeed.'

Donoghue replaced the receiver and then immediately picked it up again. He dialled an internal number.

'Collator,' said a young voice on the other end of the 'phone.

'DI Donoghue here, can you send me up the missing person file we are holding on one Flora Middleton, please?'

'I was about to send it up to you, sir.'

'You were? Did Forensic get on to you first?'

'Forensic? No, sir, the regular cross-referencing following the Maryhill Post Office raid just threw up the name. Flora Middleton is or was married to Hamish Middleton, the manager of the Post Office . . . sir? Are you still there, sir?'

'What, oh yes, send the file right up, please. Now you have a record of the registration number of the car . . . good . . . see what record we have of the car before yesterday and check the owners from now. If we haven't any information get on to the people at Swansea. I'm looking for a Middleton connection.'

'Right away, sir.'

Donoghue put the 'phone down. Thirty hours into the investigation and the case was beginning to move. Donoghue reflected that it often happened like this: after a period of deadlock or stagnation there chanced along just a whiff of suspicion, quite by accident something jarred instead of gelled. He stepped into the corridor and called, 'Ray!'

Ray Sussock came into Donoghue's office. Donoghue again noted Sussock to be looking more haggard and tired than usual. It was an appearance that Sussock normally took on when he was working late at night and when it was likely that he would be grafting right through until the morning as well. His hair was untidy, he stooped very slightly, his jaw was not quite as firmly set as it might be, his eyes seemed to protrude, but maybe that effect was caused by a certain hollowness of his cheeks. Again it was a slight hollowness, the sort a colleague or a lover might notice. But over and above the barely noticeable changes there were others; his hair was a little more dull in its greyness, his stomach was beginning to sag, there was a tired look in his eyes. Ray Sussock was, in short, looking old and Donoghue wondered whether he had been acting in Sussock's best interests in giving his approval to Sussock's request to extend his service beyond the normal retiring age. It might have been a sensible move if Sussock had been deskbound. But he hand't, he'd been at the coal face all the years, he was still there, he was, it looked like, going to remain there. And it was beginning to tell.

'Take a pew, Ray,' said Donoghue, smiling.

'Thank you, sir.' Sussock sat in the chair in front of Donoghue's desk.

'You're looking tired, Ray.'

'Been ploughing through the mug-shots, sir.' Sussock squeezed the bridge of his nose. 'Got a bit of a headache.'

'Fancy a trip out?'

'Wouldn't mind, sir.'

'Good. I'm pleased to report that there's been some progress in the form of an unusual, er, intriguing would be a better word, an intriguing link.'

'Oh?'

'Yes. Mr Hamish Middleton, the manager of the Post Office reported the disappearance of his wife some two years ago. Mrs Middleton's fingerprints, or one of them, was found in the interior of the car used as the getaway car in yesterday's raid.'

'My heavens,' said Sussock slowly. 'So she's alive and . . .'

'Well, let's not jump to conclusions, Ray. Forensic is

sending on the report, but I understand the print in question is quite old, having been preserved on an oily, dusty surface, but what we must ascertain is her connection with the getaway car, and through her what, if any, is Hamish Middleton's connection with the car which carried off monies from his Post Office. So the first thing to do is go over the ground of his wife's disappearance. I'll leave that to you.'

'How do you think I should approach it, sir?'

'Well, there are a number of ways. Let's kick the alternatives about a bit.'

'From Missing Persons, sir.' Sussock held up his I/D for Middleton's inspection.

'Missing Persons?' Sussock noticed Middleton to be nervous and shaking slightly.

'Mrs Middleton?' prompted Sussock.

'Oh yes, of course, my mind is preoccupied.'

'It is?'

'Yes. I thought you'd come about the robbery.'

'Which robbery is that, sir?'

'The Post Office robbery yesterday. I work there.'

'I see,' said Sussock.

'Well, look,' said Middleton, 'are you going to stand here all day or do you want to come in out of the rain?' There was a nervousness in his voice, especially noticeable since it had not rained all day. It was in fact a sunny, refreshing day. Sussock didn't comment, but slipped his trilby off his head and stepped into Middleton's house.

Middleton owned a white-painted bungalow which nestled in a cul-de-sac of white-painted bungalows in Bearsden. It seemed to Sussock to be a sleepy enclave in the vigorous city. The houses were not any more valuable than the terraced villas and the west end tenements of the I'm-here-and-I'm-going-even-further brigade. But here it was all south-facing windows, tweed skirts, walking sticks, and blackbirds on the cherry trees.

'You just caught me,' said Middleton. He was short and plump. A bit like his house.

'Doing what?' replied Sussock, smiling, following Middleton down his hallway.

Middleton turned and glared at him. He was about to speak and then seemed to think better of it. He indicated a room on Sussock's right. 'The living-room' he said. 'Please take a seat.' Middleton followed Sussock into the room and stooped to turn off the radio. 'I meant you caught me before I went out. I'm due to attend a meeting at the Post Office Headquarters in the city to make a report on the raid. Doubtless you have heard about the raid?'

'Yes, I did—' Sussock took out his notepad and ballpoint—'although it's not my department. I won't keep you long, Mr Middleton.'

Middleton sat in a chair opposite Sussock. There was a low coffee table between them. On the table was a large ash-tray full of cigarette ash and butts, ash also spilled on to the surface of the table. The rest of the house seemed clean, the waste bin by the fireside was empty, articles were clean and in their place. Middleton was smoking heavily.

'Your wife disappeared about two years ago?' said Sussock.

'Yes. I can't recall the exact date but it will be in your file. What is this, have you any evidence, any new evidence I mean?'

'Of what?'

'Well . . . I mean, have you any fresh information?'

'Funny you should use the word evidence,' Sussock persisted.

'I—I didn't really know what I was saying . . . I just use the word, you know, police and evidence, they go together.' Middleton grappled with a packet of cigarettes until he had extracted one. He lit it and drew on it heavily. 'Like hand and glove.'

'Or love and marriage? Crime and guilt?'

'Just what are you driving at?'

'Let's just talk about your wife.'

'I didn't like your tone, Sergeant. I won't put up with it.'

I won't put up with it. I won't put up with any more bad time-keeping, personal 'phone calls, lights left on. Sussock suddenly glimpsed Middleton, the petty tyrant in charge of the General Post Office.

'You do wish to cooperate with us in investigating your wife's disappearance?'

'Of course.' A little venomously.

'Only we'd have to start making assumptions if you didn't cooperate.'

'Now look here . . .'

'When did you last see your wife?'

'All this information is contained in your files. If you haven't come up with anything new, I can't help you because I don't have any further information.'

'This is just routine,' said Sussock. 'We don't like open cases gathering dust.'

Middleton grunted.

'I understand that you couldn't, and I presume still can't, think of a good reason for your wife's disappearance?'

'No and no.'

'No rows, arguments?'

'No, no.'

'Insurance?'

'What!'

'Was your wife insured against loss of life?'

'Yes,' said Middleton, 'she was, and I would point out that I still pay the monthly premium. The insurance company still consider her to be alive and I still consider her to be alive.'

'Do you?'

'Yes. Well, you have to, don't you?'

'Two years ago she disappeared?'

'Two years ago last August. I came home from work and she wasn't at home. She was always at home, then one day she wasn't.'

'She disappeared on a weekday?'

'A Monday, as I remember.'

'When did you report her missing?'

'Um, the following day, I think.'

'Why so late?'

'Was that late? I took advice from you people. I did 'phone the police on the Monday evening. 'Bit too early to worry, sir,' said the man to whom I spoke. 'If she's still missing tomorrow call in and we'll take some details from you?' Which is exactly what I did.'

'I see.'

'The police were very thorough. They turned my house upside down and had dogs in the back garden.'

'Any of your wife's relatives have any idea where she might have gone?'

'No.'

'Or why she might have gone?'

'Her brother came here after her disappearance and started making some fantastic allegations.'

'Such as?'

'That I murdered her.' Middleton started to chuckle and both his chins began to wobble.

'Did you?'

Middleton didn't reply. He stopped laughing.

'That's not so funny, is it, sir?' said Sussock.

'Damn right it's not,' said Middleton.

'Oh, I'm so glad we agree,' said Sussock, shutting his notebook.

DONOGHUE: Didn't lean on him too hard?

SUSSOCK: No, sir. Just enough to put him on edge. Just as you suggested.

DONOGHUE: You didn't mention the latent in the car?

SUSSOCK: No, sir.

DONOGHUE: Good. We'll keep that one up our sleeve for the time being, Ray.

SUSSOCK: I'm going to call on her brother now.

DONOGHUE: Yes, that would be the next logical move. Come straight back here and we'll chew over anything you dig up.

SUSSOCK: Yes, sir.

Sussock put the 'phone down and left the kiosk. He held the door open for the lady who had been waiting for him to finish his call.

'About six months,' said the man. He was tall and thin but muscular. He hadn't shaved that morning, his hair needed trimming. There was a worldly-wise look in his eyes. 'Coming into the house? I'm sick fed up of digging the garden.' The man drove the spade into the soil and walked down the path toward the house, leaving the spade standing vertically in the vegetable patch. Sussock followed him.

'Planting the potatoes next spring,' said the man, standing aside and letting Sussock enter his home. The man then sat on the step and tugged at his Wellington boots. 'Go straight in,' he said, looking over his shoulder. 'There's no one at home.'

Presently the man padded into the sitting-room in his stockinged feet. 'This is how I spend most of my days,' he said. 'Gardening. Digging it over a couple of times before the winter. When I was working the whole garden was a shambles; now I'm redundant, have been for a year, the patch is up to scratch, as they say.'

'No chance of a job?'

'No.' The man shook his head. 'I'm thirty-seven years old and I knew that if I wasn't fixed up within three months of getting the push then I was for the shredder. But there are dividends; no more business lunches, no meetings to prepare for, no deadlines to meet, nobody burning your ear for reports, so the blood pressure's down and the garden means the waistline is down to a respectable measurement.' He patted his stomach. 'Mind you, I keep active, that's the secret, do something constructive each day. Otherwise you'll let it get on top of you and you'll mope and spend all day watching horse-racing on the box.'

'Pity more don't have that attitude,' said Sussock.

'It's not easy.' The man sat in an armchair. 'Do sit down, Mr Sussock. You know the temptation is to let it all slide, to let go completely. I was surprised, I found it's harder to stay on top of your life when you've nothing to do than it is when you're working under pressure. When the company was fit, I used to dream about being able to spend each day fishing, but believe me, what I wouldn't give now for a room full of ringing telephones and the second-level manager going bananas. Well—' he put his hand on his knee—'tea or coffee? You're the first male company I've had for ten days.'

'Tea, please,' said Sussock, smiling as he relaxed into the armchair.

'So what's all the sudden interest in Flora?' said the man as he returned to the room with a teapot and two cups on a tray.

Sipping his tea, Sussock said, 'So it's just routine really. Don't have any new information, just going over the ground again in case we missed anything first time round.'

'That's good of you,' said the man, but he sounded disappointed.

'Can we talk about the statement she made, you say it was six months before she disappeared?'

'Well, she first told me about six months before she vanished.'

'What did she say?'

'She said, "He's going to kill me." '

'What made her say that?'

'I don't know why she said it. Why she feared it? Now that's a little different, the difference may be fine, but it's a difference. She feared it because Middleton had run up huge gambling debts. He's in GA.'

'GA?'

'Gamblers Anonymous. Flora thought he wanted to get his hands on her life assurance. She had taken out quite a big policy at his insistence some years before.'

'At his insistence?'

'So I believe. They had no children, he was older than she and the principal earner although she was a trained physiotherapist, yet he demanded she insure her life. She prevaricated a bit, she couldn't see the point, but in the end she insured against her death by accident or illness to the tune of, well, I don't recall the amount, but it was a substantial five-figure sum.'

'I see.' Sussock began taking notes.

'I told all this to the officers who called round at the time of Flora's disappearance.'

'I know, Mr Anderson,' said Sussock. 'But note-taking helps me to think. I'm an old cop. I've got old ways.'

'Well, about six months before she vanished, she told me what I just told you. Apparently he was moping and agitated and he was big enough to admit he owed money, a lot of money. Then Flora noticed that he had begun to look at her in an odd way. She said she would catch him glancing at her with the sort of look which makes you visualize little cogs turning away behind the eyes. She remembered the insurance policy she'd taken out, put two and two together and came round here. She was frightened. I told her to leave him. She wouldn't, reckoned it was daft to leave your husband because of the way he looks at you. That was in the February.

'She never stopped worrying about it and she arranged to meet the agent from the insurance company. She asked him to fix it so the company didn't pay out on her death, not pay to her husband, Middleton, that is.'

'She could have made a simple will.'

'Which is exactly what the Insurance Agent advised. He said the company could not *not* pay out, because that would be breach of contract.'

'Did she write any of this down?'

'No. She did make a will which dictates that everything, the life insurance money, her capital, all her possessions, everything in fact goes to my two daughters and to be held in Trust for them until they reach the age of twenty-one. The will does not give any reason for this, it's just a simple directive. I witnessed the will, that's how I know.'

'I see. How did her husband take to being cut out so completely?'

'He doesn't know, she didn't tell him in case it made things even worse between them.' Anderson paused. 'Middleton still thinks he's going to come into money in a few years' time when she's presumed dead.'

'Do you think she's dead?' It was a sudden question. Sussock surprised himself by asking it. Anderson managed to smile. He nodded. 'Yes, Sergeant. I think she's dead.'

'Did anything out of the ordinary happen prior to your sister's death?'

'No, nothing unusual, if you can call being convinced that your husband is about to do you in normal.'

'No fierce arguments?'

'No.'

'No fights?'

'No. She just disappeared. That is to say, she didn't pack her case and go, she took with her what she was standing in, nearest we could guess was an old pair of denims and an old blouse.'

'Last seen?'

'By me, three days before she was reported missing. Last seen by a neighbour on the Saturday morning before the Monday that she was reported missing. They chatted, her and the neighbour. Flora seemed all right, apparently. Last seen by him, Middleton, on the day before she vanished.'

'So, given the alleged threats from Hamish Middleton, the last reliable sighting of her was on the Saturday, two days before she was reported missing.'

'Yes.' Anderson nodded. He was leaning forward in the chair, resting his elbows on his knees, holding his cup with both hands. 'Forty-eight hours before she disappeared. It's a long time to do anything.'

CHAPTER 4

Friday, October 11, 4.00 p.m.

'Feelings about Middleton?' Donoghue leaned back in his chair and pulled on his pipe. The sweet-smelling smoke punched at Sussock's chest.

'Couldn't put my finger on it, sir,' said Sussock. 'But there was something I didn't like about him.'

'Try to search for it when you write your report, Ray. Explore your feelings, but try to keep prejudice at bay. Smoke bother you?'

'What? Oh no, sir.' But he couldn't stop himself from coughing.

After a short pause Donoghue asked, 'When did you last have a break, Ray?'

'Summer.'

'Any leave due?'

'Couple of days,' said Sussock. 'I'm saving time for Hogmanay.'

'Don't overwork yourself, Ray.' Donoghue took his pipe from his mouth and laid it in his ashtray. 'I like hard workers, but I have no room for martyrs. You have to know when to call it a day.'

Sussock thought, That's rich coming from you, Mr Donoghue, very rich. Then he said, 'Indeed yes, sir.'

'Well, back to the missing Flora Middleton. I want you to have this, Ray.' Donoghue passed the case file across the desk and Sussock grasped it. 'I've cross-referenced it to the Post Office snatch and my own feeling is that we'll be picking each other's brains over the next few days. We're still waiting for a response from Swansea on the history of the car, the history of ownership that is. I'll let you have all the information as soon as it comes in.'

'Very good, sir.'

'You can make a start on it tomorrow. I don't think Mrs Middleton's going anywhere.'

Sussock took the file back to his office and slipped it into his filing cabinet. He went down to the front desk and signed himself off duty. He caught a bus at George Square and arrived at Elka Willems's flat in Langside at 4.30 p.m.

'I thought you weren't coming,' she said smiling and stepped aside, holding her door open for him.

'This isn't late, not when the mighty Fabian is in the driving seat.' He kissed her as he entered her flat and shed his hat and coat.

Elka Willems owned a room and kitchen in Langside. She had decorated it in pastel shades and had managed to generate a feeling of space. The flat reminded Sussock of the home he'd grown up in, but he had been one of a family of six and their room and kitchen hadn't been in the dry and civilized Langside, it had been in the old Gorbals, the little world: the screams in the night, the blood on the stair.

Sussock smiled at her. She was wearing a full-length cotton robe, black with a red print of flowers. Her blonde hair hung around her shoulders. Sussock turned and walked into the sitting-room cum bedroom. There was a pine-framed double bed in the recess, a rubber plant by the bay window and a Van Gogh print on the wall. He sat in a chair as Elka Willems kneeled to pick up a sewing pattern which lay on the floor and, as she did so, the front of her robe fell away and Sussock saw the soft curve of her breasts.

'You look tired, Old Sussock,' she said as she walked on tiptoe across the carpet, carrying the sewing pattern and the material to a wicker box which lay by the bookcase.

'I am.' Sussock unclipped his tie; it was standard issue for policemen in the city and would come away in the hands of any thug who might try to garrotte him.

'You'd better not be that tired. I've been waiting in for you, I could have used my free time more profitably.' She crossed the room again, running her finger round his forehead as she passed behind the chair, and began to tug the curtains shut.

'I'll not disappoint you,' said Sussock. 'You know me, get better with age.'

'Well, I'd say that was true if you're anything to go by.' She walked over to the bed and let the robe fall away. For a second she stood naked and Sussock gazed at her with an awe which, if anything, had grown in the months he had been her lover. Six feet tall, slim, shapely, long blonde hair: his Nordic goddess. She slid gracefully under the duvet and Sussock turned his attention to a stubborn knot in his shoe-lace.

The man was frightened. The rap of his letter-box did not come as a surprise, but the sound made his heart miss a beat none the less. He rose slowly to his feet. His legs felt weak. He walked down the hallway and opened the door. Wee Timmy the Rat stood on the stair, smiling a thin smile beneath a thin nose and glassy eyes. Wee Timmy the Rat was a few inches shy of five feet, but he could afford to smile because behind him was Brickbat Wullie, who was built like a steam engine and who had a squashed nose and didn't seem to have a forehead. As if Brickbat Wullie wasn't insurance enough, Wee Timmy the Rat had brought along another bruiser whom the man had not seen before. He looked at the new bruiser. He could tell from the eyes that, unlike Brickbat Wullie, who did it because he was told to do it, the new boy did it because he liked it.

'Do you have my money?' Wee Timmy the Rat didn't mess about.

'Timmy,' said the man, but Wee Timmy the Rat was already shaking his head. 'I need more time, Timmy. I got it already, but I can't get at it.'

'I don't need double talk, crap and excuses.' Wee Timmy the Rat stepped aside and the bruisers advanced.

'We got the money!' The man became excited. 'Us, wait! We did the Post Office job.'

'You did?' Wee Timmy the Rat began to smile. 'Now that's smart, that's rare, but I still don't see any money. The two thousand friendly green things you promised me.'

'Two thousand . . .' The man's jaw dropped.

'Business is tough,' said Wee Timmy the Rat. 'Interest rates are high, getting higher.'

'I can get it, the cash. We just need more time.

We have to launder it.'

'So take it to the steamie.' Wee Timmy the Rat turned away and walked down the stair. 'OK, boys.'

Five minutes later the two bruisers left the man's flat and Wee Timmy the Rat returned. He went into the living-room and nodded with satisfaction at the smashed TV screen and the splintered hi-fi. Then he went into the bedroom. The mattress had been slashed. The man lay at the foot of the bed, curled up on the floor, clutching his ribs. Wee Timmy the Rat knelt down close to him. 'How long do you want?' he asked. 'Shall we say another week?'

The man nodded.

'Well, that would bring the debt up to four thousand. Four thousand friendly green things.'

The man opened his mouth. It was full of blood. He tried to speak and couldn't.

'So what's your problem?' Wee Timmy the Rat stood up and for the first time the man noticed he was wearing crocodile skin shoes. 'You've got away with quarter of a million, you can afford it. I'll see myself out.'

Later, much later, the man lowered himself into a hot bath. His body was a mass of bruises, almost as though from his neck down his skin was of a darker pigmentation. His face, neck and hands were untouched. He's clever like that is Wee Timmy the Rat, the man thought as he winced.

Saturday, October 12, 9.00 a.m.

'Came in this morning, Ray,' said Donoghue, scraping ash from his pipe bowl into his ashtray.

'Interesting,' said Sussock. He stood in the middle of the floor in Donoghue's office studying the sheet of paper. It came from the collator and gave a history of the ownership of the car used in the getaway from the Post Office raid, based on information supplied from Swansea. The car had had four owners, the last owner was Hamish Middleton, currently manager of the General Post Office in Maryhill.

'I like to keep an open mind, Ray,' said Donoghue, pulling a pipecleaner through the stem. 'Police work can make you a very suspicious person, but even I who strives with every diminishing success for big-mindedness in all things cannot help but be curious in this case.'

Sussock said, 'I think it stinks like a blocked up shit-house.'

'I'm not going to do anything at the moment.' Donoghue extracted the pipecleaner, it was slimy with brown nicotine and black tar.

'You're not? We have enough here to bring him in for questioning.'

'I know, but Middleton isn't going anywhere and I want to see if the other lines of inquiry throw up any names or information. This still might be coincidence, or it, might not, but I don't want to tip Middleton off.' He blew down the stem.

'I see.'

'This does not of course mean that your inquiry into the disappearance of Mrs Flora Middleton is in any way hampered. Just carry on as before.'

'It certainly explains why her fingerprint was found in the car.'

'Indeed, but that isn't the end of the matter.'

'No?" Sussock shuffled awkwardly.

'Ray, ask the Collator if he has any data on the car during the period when Middleton was the owner. Then take it from there. If you draw a blank come back and we'll discuss it.' Donoghue started to pat his jacket pocket, then stood and plunged his hands into his coat pocket.

'Right, sir,' said Sussock.

'Damn!' said Donoghue.

'Sir?'

'I said damn. I've left my tobacco at home.'

The Collator had nothing on the P Division records. The Police National Computer took two hours to provide information to the effect that the motor vehicle in question had been involved in a road traffic incident two years previously. A prosecution resulted in respect of one Ernest Robert Whannell. File held by the Campbeltown Police.

'Two years ago last August,' Sussock repeated the information for the benefit of the person at the other end of the 'phone, who was not deaf, but, so it seemed to Sussock, exceedingly meticulous. 'Whannell, Ernest Robert.'

'Whannell, you say?' An unmistakable Kintyre accent, clear, slow, modest.

'Yes.'

'Well, it will take me some time to look out the file. Would you care to call back?'

At 1.30 p.m. Ray Sussock picked up the 'phone on his desk, dialled 9 for an outside line and telephoned the Campbeltown Police.

'Yes, I have it before me, Detective-Sergeant,' said the clear, cool voice from Kintyre when Sussock had identified himself. 'It was an incident of drunken driving. The driver, Whannell, was found to have consumed in excess of four times the legal limit when he crashed through a gate and into a field. He broke the leg of Angus McIntyre's best heifer and the beast had to be put down.'

'When did the incident take place?'

'It took place on Sunday, August 8th, at 2.00 a.m.'

'Injuries?'

'The heifer was shot by Ronald McIntyre. It wasn't in discomfort for long.'

'I meant to the passengers in the car.'

'I see. There was only the driver. The case records

indicate he was shaken but otherwise unhurt. The car was towed to Murdo McLeod's garage where it was repaired at the request of the owner, a Mr Middleton, who had given Mr Whannell permission to drive the car that weekend.'

'Where did the accident take place?'

'I told you,' said the voice with a little irritation. 'The car crashed into Angus McIntyre's five-acre and broke one of the hind legs of his best heifer whereupon it was shot by Ronald McIntyre, his son.'

'Yes, but where is Angus McIntyre's farm in relation to Campbeltown?'

'Nowhere. The McIntyres sold up last year.'

'Where did the incident take place in relation to Campbeltown?'

'On the road to Machrihanish.'

'On the main road to Machrihanish?'

'On the only road to Machrihanish.'

'I see. At the time of the incident was Whannell driving towards Campbeltown or away from it?'

'He was driving towards Campbeltown.'

'Do you have an address for Whannell?'

'I do, yes, it's dated at the time of the incident. We haven't been asked for the file so I dare say it's his last known address. It is c/o Clark, 52 Clouston Street. He appeared at Campbeltown Sheriff Court on the day after the incident and was sentenced to three months' imprisonment. There were similar previous convictions, do you see?'

'I see. Thank you very much.'

'No problem.'

Barlinnie Prison in Glasgow accommodates prisoners on remand and the hard cases waiting to be transferred to Peterhead. It also takes those sentenced to terms of twelve months or less. Mostly it's full of neds, wasters and two-time losers. It was certain to be the pokey where

Whannell was sent. Sussock dialled through to Records. Whannell had been there. He got out in two months. His discharge address was 52 Clouston Street, Glasgow 20.

Clouston Street cuts a deep canyon through four-storey sandstone tenements. In Clouston Street older-established professional people live, as do the families of younger professionals. In the street also live the elderly and the isolated, the labouring Irish sleeping five or six to a room, young men and women on the dole, having children to force the Council into giving them a home and to boost their weekly welfare cheque. There are drug addicts, drug pushers, there are thieves, pimps, pornographers, lesbians, homosexuals and prostitutes. Clouston Street is about a quarter of a mile long.

Sussock stepped into the close of No. 52 and stopped. He felt insecure. He had lived in Glasgow all his life and for most of the time he had been a cop. He was accustomed to visiting people's houses and had developed a sensitivity to a dangerous building. Such buildings have a silence all their own, punctuated occasionally by flakes of plaster and pieces of grit falling down the stair, as hundreds of tons of masonry and timber and metal twist and turn and settle by a fraction of an inch. Outside, the flakes of masonry fall more thickly and even an untrained eye can spot a bulge in the wall. Sussock stepped back on to the pavement and looked at the façade of No. 52. It was a four-storey tenement, flats front and rear of a central stair, perhaps sixteen flats in all unless there were also single ends on each landing. The wall of the building appeared vertical and solid. It made Sussock feel a little more comfortable, so he stepped back into the close. On the wall someone had written: 'To those who leave their garbage here—find another flat.' He started up the stair. It was a self-supporting stair of thin stone which angled round the square shaft in the centre of the building.

Between the second and third floors the thin metal rail had fallen away and had been replaced by a cat's cradle of nylon cord and lengths of twine. Sussock walked nearer the wall. On the third floor landing, where the flagstones lay unevenly, he noticed a door with 'Clark' painted on it and below 'Clark' were half a dozen more names written on a sheet of paper. Nothing unusual there; it was like the front of every other door on the stair, including the one-room single ends. Sussock scrutinized the list; Whannell was not one of the names. He rapped on the door anyway.

It was answered by a young man with bleary eyes. Sussock didn't think he was a night shift worker, he had answered the door too quickly and was showing too much interest. He seemed more likely to be long-term unemployed, sleeping away the day of which Sussock's visit was the high point. The man looked to be about twenty-two.

'Mr Clark?' said Sussock.

The man shook his head. 'He's no' here. You the social, aye?'

'Police.'

'Oh. Only wee Sarah in the back room is expecting the social. Clark is the factor, he disnae live here.'

'Looking for a guy called Whannell.'

The man shook his head. 'Nobody here by that name. Nobody by that name has been here since I've been here.'

'How long is that?'

'Six, seven months.'

'How many live here, in this flat?'

'Nine. Two kids.'

'Eleven in all?'

'Nine in all.'

'None of the others know him?'

The man turned like a big sloth and knocked on the first door in the corridor. 'Jim!' he shouted. The corridor was long, the ceiling high, in its heyday the flat would probably have been the home of a banker and his family. Now it was crumbling. Sussock could see into a room at the end of the corridor. There was an old cooker standing next to a double bed.

'If anyone knows him old Jim will,' said the young man. 'Sure you're not the social, no?'

'Quite positive,' said Sussock.

'Aye, only Sarah's been expecting a visit from the social for two weeks. She's not getting the money through. She has to keep going up for a counter payment.'

The door opened and an old man stepped into the corridor. He looked a bit dazed. He had mottled skin which hung in folds under his eyes and chin. He managed a weak smile for Sussock.

'Jim.'

The old man looked at the young man.

'Polis, Jim. Looking for a guy called Whannell.'

'Whannell?' said the man in a rasping voice.

'Aye, Whannell.' The young man turned to Sussock. 'We look after old Jim. Don't we, Jim?'

'Aye, you look after me, son,' said Jim. He didn't have any teeth.

'Jim's part of the flat,' said the young man. 'Used to be in the Merchant Navy. Still got that shark's tooth, Jim?'

'Whannell?' growled Sussock.

'Who?' rasped Jim.

'Whannell,' said the young man. 'Remember a guy called Whannell living here?'

'Nope,' said Jim.

'Jim's been living here since—how long have you been living in that room, Jim?'

'Thirty-seven years,' said Jim. He smiled like it was a big achievement.

Sussock said, 'Christ!' and didn't care who heard him.

'Used to be a Whannell living up the stair,' rasped the old man.

'When?'

'Nineteen-seventy-two,' said the man.

When Sussock was going down the stair the young man leaned on the railings and said, 'If you should happen to see the social, chief . . .'

Sussock turned and stared at him.

'Only Sarah's been waiting.'

Outside the wind had changed and the city smelled of dead cats. It tends to do so from time to time.

'It's about time you took an interest,' said the man in tweeds. 'Still, I won't complain too much. Sure you won't have a drink? Little short for the road?'

'No, thank you,' said King.

'Well, not much to add. Local boys came round, took a shuftie. Went into the garden, came back into the house, went out again. Went away promising action and everything under the sun. Haven't heard a word from them since. That was six months ago.'

'I'm sure they did everything they could, sir,' said King.

'I'm sure they did.' The man began to rock backwards and forwards on his heels. 'But it wasn't enough, was it, young man? Didn't get my bloody guns back, did I? Didn't see hide nor hair of them, did I?'

King glanced about him, the large windows, the expanse of polished wooden floor, the oak table with Queen Anne legs, the shelves from floor to ceiling filled with books. 'Colonel Bushell will receive you in the library, sir,' said the man in the collar and tails. 'If you would care to follow me, sir.'

And King had obediently followed.

'What was stolen, sir? Two shot-guns and a hunting rifle? Is that it?'

'It's enough. Two Purdy twelve-bores, fine guns, two antique pistols, did you get those down?'

'Yes, I have a note, sir.'

'And my Mauser.'

'It's the Mauser I'm particularly interested in,' said King.

'Got a lead, eh?'

'Probably.'

'Good-oh.'

'Can you describe it, sir?'

'Well, basically it was a German Mauser rifle, Second War vintage. Excellent rifle but experts say that our own Lee Enfield 303 has the edge over it. Well, my gun had been what the Yanks call "sporterized", clumsy term, but it means that the original stock had been changed to a smoother, lighter type, with a sort of pistol grip. There was a hole in the new stock through which you put your thumb. Didn't like it at first, but I had to admit it was a damn comfortable way of holding a rifle. Sights modified and I had telescopic attachments as well.'

'Was any ammunition stolen, sir?'

'For the Mauser, yes, twelve rounds.'

As he drove away from the castle, King stopped just before the bend in the drive and looked back. A grey-white building with turrets and towers, pine woods at each side, an expanse of lawn before, the hills behind. Above the hills, the deep dark blue bank of clouds of an impending storm. King turned and fastened his seat-belt. Perth to Glasgow, two hours at the outside. The rear wheels spun on the gravel as he let in the clutch.

'Probably was his rifle, sir,' said King when he returned to P Division, well within the two hours. 'He couldn't tell me anything about the break-in that wasn't contained in the file at the local nick.'

'But you think it's his rifle,' asked Donoghue. He leaned backwards in his chair and sucked on his empty pipe.

'I think so, sir. Without any way of telling and proceeding on an emotional level, I think it was his rifle that was used in the Post Office raid. Not many hunting rifles are stolen, his antique pistols and the shot-guns could be disposed of through shady retail outlets, but the hunting rifle, much modified at that, I think could only have been disposed of in the underworld.'

'I think you're right. Now what?'

'Well, sir, I would think that anyone trying to unload flintlock pistols and high class shot-guns into gunsmiths or antique-dealers could lead us to the raiders, assuming the guns are all part of the same haul.'

'Anything to be done?'

'I don't know. The Tayside Region Police circulated a description of the guns, plus their serial numbers. Mind you, I dare say a reminder wouldn't do any harm.'

'Better get on with it then,' said Donoghue. 'Oh, and don't forget to write it up for the file.'

'Feeling all right?' asked Montgomerie.

'Me?' said Bell. 'Yeah, sure, I'm OK.'

'You've been looking uncomfortable all day.'

'Indigestion,' said Bell.

'You'll not be in for a pint after work, then?'

'After work? You mean this slave driver does let you go home after all?'

'Fabian?' Montgomerie smiled. 'Only sometimes. Most times you have to sneak out of the back door when he's not looking. Are you coming for a drink, then?'

'Me, no, not tonight, thanks. I'm meeting some friends.'

'OK, some other time. So what's Fabian been having you do today then, Ding-Dong?'

'Mug-shots,' growled Bell. 'Me and young Abernethy. Books full of them. After a while one face just merges into another. That's why I came down here for a coffee.'

'Gives the new boys all the menial tasks, does Fabian,' said Montgomerie. 'Always has. Anyway we might have cracked the case.'

'We have!' Bell looked up suddenly.

'Good news, isn't it? I don't know the details, but apparently Ray Sussock got a lead on the car.'

'He did?'

'Yes, came about through a Missing Persons file, I believe. There's a link of sorts with the Post Office job. I don't know any details.'

'Oh,' said Bell. Then: 'You know I've never worked with a DI like this. The man's a Zealot.'

'He's straight.'

'You ever crossed him?'

'Once or twice,' admitted Montgomerie.

'Hard man.'

'Straight,' said Montgomerie. He rose from his seat and went from the small room called the 'canteen' to the kitchen, washed his mug and went back upstairs to the CID rooms.

In the evening, in the dim room, the meeting started. The man stood. His wooden chair scratched against the floor and he coughed to clear his throat. The others sat quite still and formed a circle about him.

'I was young when I began,' he said. 'I was still not yet twenty.'

Somebody in the room drew breath between his teeth. The man faltered. Why did he do that, he thought, why did he unnerve me like that? He must know how hard it is. He's heard me say this before, it can't surprise him? 'I was not then twenty,' he repeated.

Then there was silence. It was a heavy silence and louder for the other man having drawn breath between his teeth. The man paused, he would not stumble, not this time, not fumble this time, no. He looked at the naked light-bulb and the single gas-ring and the collection of white enamel cups on the table by the door.

After, they would gather at the ring and boil water to slop over the instant coffee powder which lay in the bottom of the cups. One cup each with powdered milk and a little sugar, the secretary would read the notices, any visitors or newcomers would be welcomed. Then they would disperse, some in cars, some on public transport, others would walk. This night the man was the first to speak. He knew it was always harder if you were kicking off, everybody listens to the first speaker. By the time they get round the circle everybody is lost in remorse and mulling over their thoughts too much to take notice of the last man.

'It's the thrill of not knowing,' said the man. 'It's not the winning or the losing. The result is unimportant, but it's the thrill of not knowing, throwing everything to chance, taking the risk . . . It's cost me a lot, not just in money. I was married, my wife left me. My savings were gambled away. I had to sell my house and move from Edinburgh. I rent a small flat now. It started with a five-pound bet at the bookies', a five-pound line on a nag that couldn't lose. I lost most of what I gambled. I needed money to live. I went to the moneylenders.'

The same man whistled again.

'Just a one-off loan, that's what I wanted. But they've got their teeth into me . . . I have done something stupid. I have done something very stupid.' Then he sank back into his chair and buried his face in his hands.

The woman sitting next to him put her hand on his shoulder and said, 'Do you want to tell us, friend? Share it with us, brother.' But the man would not be drawn and so the woman stood and began to speak.

Outside the hall the man who spoke first was approached by a shorter, older man who said, 'We have to talk.' The man pulled his arm away and said, 'No, no, no.'

Later that night the man left his lodgings and walked

to the public telephone kiosk. He waited until five minutes past midnight, the pre-arranged time which indicated he was talking freely, and then made the call. It was answered on the seventeenth ring, the agreed signal that the recipient of the call was also free to talk. The man said, 'They're on to the car.' Then he hung up.

CHAPTER 5

Sunday, October 13, 10.00 a.m.

'So that's about it,' said Sussock. He sat in front of Donoghue's desk. Donoghue, sitting behind the desk rested his elbows on the blotter and steepled his fingers beneath his chin. He looked at Sussock and said nothing.

'The car was in the Campbeltown area on the weekend that Mrs Middleton disappeared,' said Sussock. Again Donoghue remained silent.

'It was owned by her husband, the car was. It was driven by a man called Whannell. I am still trying to trace him, Whannell that is.' Sussock began to feel very edgy. Review meetings were not his favourite part of policework. Especially hastily assembled meetings which took place amid great resentment on a Sunday morning, when it was raining outside, when at either side of him sat the bright young PCs patiently listening while he, the old boy of the team, fumbled with embarrassment. His unease was compounded by the presence of Elka Willems, who sat at the end of Donoghue's desk wearing a crisp white shirt with her hair in a bun. She kept her head bowed and wrote on her pad.

'Go on, Ray,' Donoghue said.

'I—er—we know that Mrs Middleton was in the car at some point. We can't be certain she was in the car that weekend.'

'Can we assume so?'

'There's no reason why she should be.'

'You think not?' Donoghue lowered his hands and drummed his fingers on the table and fixed Sussock with a stare. 'Are you assuming that the car was driven to the bottom of the Kintyre Peninsula by Whannell, and by Whannell alone?'

'Yes.'

'Because there was no one else involved in the accident?'

'Yes.'

'Cargo?'

'Sir?'

'Cargo, Ray. Was the car carrying anything?'

'At the time of the accident, no, it wasn't.'

'Before?'

'It could well have been.'

'Could well have been, you say.' Donoghue paused. 'All right, we don't have any evidence so let's work on an assumption.'

'Dangerous, sir.'

'Probably, but I can't see any other way forward. But having said that, we'll retain an open mind. So the car when owned by Middleton is known to have been in a reasonably remote part of Scotland on the weekend that Mrs Middleton disappeared. Now that is a significant fact that Middleton kept from the police investigation of two years ago. He freed himself from suspicion by being obvious, by keeping a high profile that weekend. But nobody noticed that his car was missing. So already we have something to be suspicious about. Point two: Middleton's car was driven by one Whannell. What is the connection between Middleton and Whannell?'

'Unknown fact, sir.'

'All right. What is known about Whannell? He went down for the drinking and driving offence in

Campbeltown because he had previous convictions. What were those convictions—all road traffic offences?'

'Not all,' conceeded Sussock. 'In fact I know Whannell from way back. He has two assaults to severe injury, one reset, numerous breaches of the peace.'

'So our suspicions are aroused by the nature of the relationship between the manager of the Post Office and a wee thug like Whannell, especially when Whannell drove Middleton's car on the weekend that Mrs Middleton disappeared. Our suspicions are further aroused when that same man, Middleton, has his Post Office knocked over and the raiders disappear from the face of the earth, this time taking a quarter of a million pounds with them.

'But to return to events two years ago on the lonely, pasty-looking stretch of road between Campbeltown and Machrihanish. Did it not strike you as peculiar that a man alone in a car at two in the forenoon was drunk?'

'Frankly no, sir,' said Sussock.

'It wouldn't be unusual in Glasgow, but does Whannell have any known associates in Kintyre? Why should an overgrown ned from the city be drunk in a lonely part of Scotland at two a.m.? His usual drinking pattern might well be that he locks himself away with his mates in a room and kitchen for a three-day bender. Now, did the crash take place when the car was travelling to or from Campbeltown?'

'He was driving towards Campbeltown.'

'He was therefore driving away from Machrihanish.'

'Yes, sir.'

'Now, why might he have been drinking?'

'Because he was agitated about something,' said Sussock, sitting upright. 'I think I see what you're leading up to. There's an earlier Machrihanish connection, a trace of a rare plant which was found in Middleton's car, and there's a small colony of this particular plant near

Machrihanish, Cabbage something . . .'

'Sea Cabbage,' said Donoghue turning the pages of the file. '*Brassica oleracea*.'

'It flowered at the time of year that Whannell was in the area and the plant spore in the rear of the car had flowered.'

Elka Willems raised her head and smiled at Sussock.

'Straight after the meeting, Ray,' said Donoghue, 'you'd better get on the 'phone to the police at Campbeltown and tell them that there's a body buried near Machrihanish.'

Sussock nodded. 'Indeed, indeed,' he said.

'So for action—' Donoghue turned to Elka Willems—'DS Sussock to liaise with the Campbeltown Police to examine the possibility of Mrs Middleton having been murdered and her body buried near Machrihanish. DS Sussock to continue the search for Whannell, in connection with Mrs Middleton's disappearance. Don't approach Middleton without consulting me first, Ray.'

'Right,' said Sussock.

'Abernethy, Bell? Mugshots. Anything turn up?'

'No,' said Bell shortly.

Abernethy shook his head. 'We couldn't match anything with the description given, sir.'

Donoghue nodded, 'Nice, precise but full answer.' He looked coldly at Bell, then turned to King and raised his eyebrows.

'We checked records and discovered that a hunting rifle had been stolen from a castle in Perthshire about six months ago. It was part of a larger haul of guns, two valuable shot-guns and two antique pistols. We're trying to get a line on the rifle via the other weapons. I've alerted all the major antique-dealers in Scotland, the gunsmiths as well.' King paused. 'Well, that's about it,' he said. 'I'm still working on it.'

'Good. Montgomerie?'

'The reconstruction has not yet produced any further witnesses,' said Montgomerie, who, even when sitting, had a stomach so flat a ruler could be laid across it. He faltered, he was nervous in Donoghue's company. He sensed that Donoghue did not like him, and he further sensed that Donoghue knew Montgomerie knew he was not being allowed any quarter.

'So you've nothing to report,' said Donoghue.

'No,' conceded Montgomerie. 'But I would submit that that is relevant.'

Donoghue looked at Montgomerie and nodded. 'I'll accept that,' he said. 'So to be minuted for action, King to pursue any lead following the guns being stolen from the castle in Perthshire. Hobnobbing with the rich, eh, King?'

'Absolutely, sir,' said King.

'Bell, since the mugshots turned up nothing for us to go on, I'd like you to avail yourself to DS Sussock.'

'Would that mean me going to Campbeltown?' Bell asked.

'It would indeed.'

Bell made to speak, as if in protest, but in the event said nothing.

'Minute that DC Bell will assist DS Sussock, please,' said Donoghue.

Elka Willems scribbled on her pad.

'That would be just the job,' said Sussock. 'Two single rooms, say for two nights, dare say it wouldn't be difficult to extend our stay if necessary. Campbeltown isn't exactly overrun with tourists at this time of the year.'

'It isn't exactly overrun with tourists at any time of the year,' said the voice on the other end of the line. 'As to resources, we have one sniffer dog, she more than works for her keep.'

'You get a lot of buried bodies?'

'We get a few people disappearing on the eastern shore of the Mull, very rocky, strong tides, the dog comes in handy when we are searching the shore.'

'Well, I think we'll be able to pinpoint the search area to a few square yards after we've found the cabbage.'

'The what?'

'The Sea Cabbage.'

'I didn't know there was such a plant.'

'Oh, didn't you?' said Sussock with a gentle hint of authority in his voice. 'Actually it's quite rare and usually grows south of the border, but there's a small colony on the west shore of the Mull, near Machrihanish.'

'It will be in the dunes, then?'

'The dunes?'

'Aye, the sand dunes there, they are quite high, steep-sided, mostly covered with Marram grass. I'm sure we can find your cabbage if you tell us what it looks like.'

'Ah,' said Sussock.

'You don't know?' said the voice, seizing quickly on Sussock's hestitation.

'Oh, I know what it looks like in August,' Sussock replied after some quick thinking. 'It flowers in August.'

'That is not a great help to us in the October of the year, Detective-Sergeant. Unless of course you'd care to wait until August next year. It will be a little warmer for a walk on the dunes too, it's a wicked bit of coastline in the winter. It's bleak enough, do you see?'

'Yes, I see,' said Sussock. 'We'll need to be wrapped up, then?'

'Oh yes. And a pair of good walking boots.'

'Walking boots. That could pose a problem.'

'I wouldn't recommend you to walk on the dunes in city shoes.'

'I'll certainly follow your recommendation,' said Sussock. 'I'll see you tonight, then.'

'About seven-thirty or eight. The other officer's name?'

'DC Bell.'

'Thank you. Good day.'

Sussock put the 'phone down and said, 'Walking boots.' He picked up the 'phone again and dialled an internal number. Montgomerie answered the 'phone. 'CID rooms.'

'Bell there?' asked Sussock.

'Just nipped out of the room, Sarge.'

'When he comes back, will you tell him that we leave for Campbeltown at four p.m. today. He can take time out to pack a suitcase, say enough for three days, and tell him he'll need a pair of walking boots.'

'Will do, Sarge. Nice for some, isn't it, a walking holiday in Kintyre while the workers stay and graft in the city.'

'Just tell him, Montgomerie.'

Sussock hung up. He put his coat on and left his office, carrying his trilby in one hand and his gloves in the other. He signed out and as he walked away from the police station he put on hat and gloves and strode out purposefully. He walked around the corner to the police garage and booked out an unmarked car. He drove as purposefully as he had walked, but it was a show, bravado, he was weak at the knees and felt hollow inside. Sussock drove to the south side and pulled the car up at the kerb outside a modest house in Rutherglen. He left the car and walked down the driveway of the house and, as he did so, a small woman with hurried movements and pinched face saw his approach. She left the garden and fled into the house.

Sussock approached the back door through which the woman had entered the house and tapped on the door with his knuckles. Already he felt tired. There was no answer to his knock and so he tapped the door again. Eventually he banged on the door with the flat of his hand.

An upstairs window above the door opened and the shrew poked her head out. 'What do you want?' She spat the words.

'Just my hiking boots,' said Sussock wearily.

'Going hiking, are you, doesn't surprise me, didn't really like work, did you? Couldn't provide a decent standard of living for me an' Samuel, could you?'

'Are you going to let me in?'

'I can't,' said the woman. There were heavy lines on her forehead. 'Samuel's brought a new friend home with him. You'll just embarrass him like you always do. If you don't go away I'll call the police.'

'Go right ahead,' said Sussock. 'It's still my house.'

'Half of it is,' she replied venomously.

'All of it is. It is still in my name. The law demands that you shall have half and half you shall have, as soon as the divorce is finalized. But right now if you don't open the door I'll break in through the window.'

'That's the sort of thing you'd do, isn't it?'

'Yes.'

'You wait there, I'll let Samuel bring them down for you.'

'They're in the small room where the rest of my things are stacked . . .' But the small woman had already shut the window.

They kept Sussock waiting for fifteen minutes. Then the door opened and a young man with a black T-shirt, baggy trousers and plimsolls stood on the step holding a pair of battered hiking boots in a well-manicured hand from which all hair had been removed.

'Here you are, Daddy.' He smiled a thin contemptuous smile.

'Took you long enough to find them.' Sussock snatched his boots.

'Oh, we found them quickly, me and Paul. Paul's my new friend. But then Mummy took a funny turn, she was upset by you arriving on our doorstep, so we made her a cup of tea to calm her down.'

Sussock turned and walked away.

'Oh, Daddy,' the young man called after him. 'Mummy says I have to tell you that you were never any good to me and her.'

Sussock drove to the west end of the city and let himself into a large house with an array of bells and names on the front door. He climbed the stairs to the second floor and let himself into his bed-sit. His home, one room, rented by the month, furnished by the landlord. Some home for a man in his mid-fifties, a man who was about to retire, living here among the students and oddballs. He threw clean but unironed clothes into a suitcase and, as he did so, he told himself that it wasn't all bad, he did have the love of the strikingly beautiful Elka Willems, his marital home was soon to be sold and even half its value would be sufficient to buy a room and kitchen like Elka's, maybe even in Langside, like Elka's.

Elka Willems finished the morning shift at 2.00 p.m. She signed out at 2.30 p.m., and when she arrived home at 3.00 p.m. Ray Sussock was sitting in her close reading the Sunday newspapers. He remained with her until shortly before 4.00 p.m. when he drove back to P Division to collect DC Bell before proceeding to Campbeltown.

Malcolm Montgomerie was duty officer. He finished his coffee and then went from the CID rooms to the front desk in response to the 'phone-call he had received. Constable Hamilton was at the desk and Sergeant Rafferty sat at the table behind the desk. Montgomerie stood next to Hamilton.

'This lady here, sir,' said Phil Hamilton, indicating a plump woman who sat on the plastic chair in the corner of the reception area. 'Mrs McGregor.'

Montgomery lifted the hinging section of the desk and walked into the reception area. 'Mrs McGregor?' he said. 'Would you care to step this way, please?' He escorted Mrs McGregor to one of the interview rooms.

'To let you understand,' said the woman as she sat in one of the chairs and before Montgomerie had shut the door of the room. 'We have a wee problem. I've been to the social who sent me to the welfare who said I should come here to you. Well, it's my man, he's in a mess, he's got in with the moneylenders.'

Montgomerie groaned.

'You know what it means then, sir?'

'Yes,' said Montgomerie. He opened his pad and laid it on the desk. 'We know about the loan sharks, but I have to warn you that prosecuting them is difficult, most people are afraid to give evidence.'

'I know. I don't think my man will give evidence. He's a frightened man.'

'You'd better let me have some details,' said Montgomerie. 'You're Mrs McGregor?'

'Yes. Florence McGregor.'

'Your husband is?'

'Tom McGregor.'

'Age?'

'We're both thirty-five.'

'Does he work?'

'No. He hasn't seen work for five years. He probably never will, he's a time-served electrician and when he goes for a job he gets turned down because he's too old. Too old at thirty-five.'

'Where do you stay?'

The woman gave an address in Cadder.

'Well now, what exactly is happening, Mrs McGregor?'

'Och, Tom, he's in with they moneylenders, him and many others. We were short one week so we borrowed, the social security doesn't go far, sir. We couldn't pay it back, not with the interest they charged. They're waiting for Tom each day he collects his benefit and they walk him and the others from the social to the Post Office and when he cashes it they take their cut. This week was bad, the Post Office was shut, that robbery, and they walked miles in the rain to the next one. He came home soaked to the skin with half the week's money taken by the moneylenders.'

She pulled a handkerchief from her handbag and buried her face in it.

Montgomerie waited for a few moments and then prodded gently. 'So your husband and other men are escorted from the DHSS to the Post Office each giro day by the moneylenders?'

'Aye.' The woman took a deep breath. 'We've been paying back for weeks and we still owe twice what we borrowed. There's no end to it.'

'Do you know who's behind this particular money-lending racket?'

'Aye,' said the woman. 'It's a wee fellow they call Wee Timmy the Rat. He's got some big guys to back him up.'

'You know those big guys?'

'Aye. They're up to their ears in debt to Wee Timmy the Rat. That's how he works, forces people to work for him rather than hire them. They pay off their debt like that. He'll be recruiting my husband next, then what'll happen? Does he have to turn criminal just because the DHSS doesn't give us enough to live on?'

'Do you think your husband might yet give evidence? I think on the face of it this is a clear-cut case of extortion.'

'You'll have to ask him. He's frightened, but there's a man stays in the next close to us. He refused to pay any money to Wee Timmy the Rat and they carved him in the back close, they cut his face off, his face was lying next to his head when they had finished, they carried him and his face to hospital, separately. See him now, his face is like a jigsaw puzzle, nearly two hundred stitches it took. But that's not the damage, the damage is inside his head. He's a broken man, his nerve has gone, he's a big guy but he's got no nerve left. He dare not leave his house and me and another woman get his messages in for him.'

Montgomerie nodded. 'I remember that incident.' So that was the handiwork of Wee Timmy the Rat, was it?'

'Aye.'

'You see, we couldn't do anything because that man wouldn't give evidence.'

'I don't think my man will. If we ask for police protection you say you can't do anything until something happens. Bit late then, isn't it?'

'We can't follow everybody who gets threatened, Mrs McGregor. If your husband could give us a statement, then on that basis the Fiscal could frame a charge against this animal. No one need find out until the trial, then we'd offer protection.'

'Only for the duration of the trial. So what happens after you get what you want, what happens to us then? What happens when his mates kick our door down at three o'clock in the morning? What happens when he gets out of gaol?'

'I'm very sympathetic, Mrs McGregor, but you have to see it from our point of view. We may, and I emphasize may, we may be able to offer protection, we can and will support your application for re-housing in another part of the city if you feel that your safety is threatened. But nothing can be done by us to stop this man unless somebody is willing to give evidence for the prosecution.'

'So you can't help us?'

'Not unless you can help us.'

'It was nae use coming here.'

'Where does this fellow hang out? Where could I see him?'

'To talk to? Is that what you're going to do, wag

a finger in his face?'

'That's up to me. At the moment I'd be happy to get a look at him.'

'You'll not say anything about me calling here? I mean, even my husband doesn't know I'm here, that's how I waited till Sunday, he calls on his mother on Sunday.'

'I won't tell him anything.'

'You could try watching for him in a bar called Dooley's, it's on Maryhill Road, near the bus garage.'

'I know it.'

'He's in there most nights. He's a little guy, spectacles, leather jacket, not like a biker, but Italian style, stinks of easy money.'

'Age?'

'Difficult to say.'

'Under thirty or over thirty?'

'Barely twenty, I'd say,' said Mrs McGregor.

Nearer twenty-five, thought Montgomerie. He raised his glass to his mouth, sipped the whisky and lowered the glass again to the table. You had to look hard to see the age, but it was there all right in his eyes and in the way he moved. All the same Montgomerie could see why Mrs McGregor had thought he was younger, the overall visual impression of Wee Timmy the Rat was of a precocious smoothie, just out of school and trying to run with the men. But it was those very same men, the hard men, who moved aside for him when he walked up to the gantry. And it wasn't the sort of bar where you would take a girl. The chairs were hard, the thin tables were sticky and hadn't been wiped for a couple of days. Cigarette ash spilled from the ashtray and mixed with the slops. The floor was covered in large red and white tiles laid out in a check pattern and it looked like it hadn't been cleaned for a couple of years. The TV above the spirit rack competed with the juke-box next to the door. It seemed to be a men only bar; not that the landlord had issued an illegal rule to that effect, just that women voted with their feet. The punters seemed to be dressed in old clothes, oily jackets with torn elbows, baggy shiny trousers, holes in the shoes. And right in the middle of it all, demanding and getting a lot of personal floor space, was Wee Timmy the Rat, light brown leather jacket, neatly pressed trousers and shiny shoes with gold buckles.

Wee Timmy the Rat sank another couple of drinks and then left the bar. Montgomerie followed. Wee Timmy the Rat walked down the Maryhill Road and went into an old close. Montgomerie edged into the close just far enough to verify that Wee Timmy the Rat was in fact climbing the stair and hadn't nipped into the back court to shake the tail. Montgomerie leaned against the dusty close wall and listened to the small man climb the stairs with a scuff of the sole of his shoes on each stair. When he reached the third floor the man stopped and Montgomerie heard the jangling of a key ring and the unlocking of at least three locks.

Montgomerie left the close, crossed over Maryhill Road and looked up the tenement. There was a light in every flat. Montgomerie concentrated on the third floor, which seemed to comprise two large flats on either side of the stair and a single end between the flats. Presently Wee Timmy the Rat appeared at the window of the left-hand flat and tugged the curtain shut. Montgomerie crossed back over the road and climbed the stair. According to the nameplate on the door three up left, Wee Timmy the Rat's surname was Sloan. Montgomerie went back down the stair: he had a name, he had an address and he had a tip-off.

He had left the close and was walking with increasing rapidity towards Dooley's Bar when he finally figured that the scream was coming from the other direction. He turned and ran, turned down a side street. There were a couple of punters hanging about, they didn't appear to be particularly concerned about the noise. Montgomerie came across a back lane running behind the middens and courts and tenements, and parallel to Maryhill Road. Down the lane a couple of neds were giving a woman the sort of attention she couldn't use.

'Police!' Montgomerie yelled and started to run towards the fray. The neds let the girl drop and started to square up to Montgomerie. They stood fast until they saw that he was six feet tall and was coming on like he meant it. Then they bolted. He let them go and helped the woman to her feet. She was shaken, maybe a little bruised, a couple of slight lacerations. She seemed to be in her mid-twenties.

'You OK?' asked Montgomerie.

'I think so.' The woman looked up at Montgomerie and he saw her eyes widen with undisguised interest. 'Just a bit bruised,' she said.

'What happened?'

'They jumped me.' She sounded educated, not especially classy, but someone who had read more than a few books. 'I don't know them, they pushed me around, groped a bit. Would have done more if you hadn't come along.'

'Do you want me to take you home? My car's just round the corner.'

'Oh no, really,' said the woman. 'I'm not damaged.'

'Sure?'

'Sure. Tell you what I would like, I mean if you're offering half an hour of your time, and that's a drink. A stiff one.'

So he took her to the Belfast Packet on the riverside.

'Smooth bar,' she said, sliding into her seat and then leaning forward, looking keenly into Montgomerie's eyes.

'I like it here,' said Montgomerie. 'It's quiet.' He too was leaning forward. He reckoned this damsel in distress could trace her lineage back to Helen of Troy.

The waitress approached. She had a red shirt and split thigh skirt.

'Lager for me, please,' said Montgomerie, 'and . . .'

'Gin and tonic,' said the woman, smiling a warm genuine smile. Montgomerie liked that.

'Double if you wish,' he said.

The woman shook her head. 'No, thanks, maybe I can have a second one later.'

'I was counting on it,' he said.

'I'm Malcolm Montgomerie.'

'My name's Sarah Whittaker.'

The first silence.

'What is it you do, Sarah, workwise I mean.'

'Nothing. Unemployed graduate. Know anybody who wants to hire a degree in Spanish Studies, two years old, no work experience?'

'It's not an uncommon problem.'

'I guess not.'

'What were you doing in Maryhill?'

'Leafleting.'

'For?'

'The Green Party.'

'That's a new one on me.'

'Political pressure group, ecology orientated, preserve the countryside, recycle waste, that sort of thing. Anti-blood sport, of course.'

'Of course.'

'What do you do?'

'I'm a fascist pig.'

Sarah Whittaker's jaw dropped.

'I'm a cop,' he added with a smile.

She returned his smile. She was attractive in a mature sort of way. Not pretty but beautiful, at least to Montgomerie's taste, with long black hair. The dim lights of the bar were just strong enough to pick out a ridge on her nose. Spectacles for reading, thought Montgomerie.

The waitress brought the drinks and Montgomerie paid her. Sarah Whittaker sipped her drink. She seemed to have recovered from her ordeal very quickly. 'Do you always work late, Malcolm?'

'Not unless I can avoid it.' He swallowed his lager.

'You don't talk like any of the cops I've met. Not that I've met a lot.'

'What do you mean?'

'You're smoother in your manner, you have a clearer voice.'

'The lingering effect of legal training.' He smiled. 'I read law at Edinburgh. I was going to be an advocate, I'd have been earning ten times the money I get now if I had stuck at it.'

'Why didn't you?'

'I didn't like the advocates I met. Some of the junior advocates used to tutor us in certain aspects of the law. I found them a smug, self-satisfied bunch without much comprehension of what life is about, not that I knew much at the time. Law seemed to be a very isolated and insulated profession, arguing guilt and innocence on academic points and forgetting about the poor guy in the dock. Wasn't for me. So I came home, back to this magnificent city of G., and started to work for her. My civic duty. I'm not that good a cop. I've made my mistakes, but I don't have any regrets.'

'So you're not a fascist at all.'

'We get labelled.'

'You know, Malcolm,' said Sarah Whittaker, 'I owe you quite a lot for what you did tonight.' Then she raised her glass and looked at him in the way a woman sometimes can. When he bought her another drink she raised her glass and said:

> 'Here's to me and one other,
> And may that other when he drinks,

Think of himself and one other,
And may that other be me.'

Then she smiled.

This made Montgomerie feel an odd sensation. His flesh and blood remained seated but his spirit momentarily went to sit at the next table. When spirit and body were again rejoined he said, 'That's nice,' because he couldn't think of anything else to say, and because he was more preoccupied with an alarm bell which was ringing in a dark recess of his mind.

'It's Captain Oates's toast,' said Sarah Whittaker. 'You know—"I'm just going outside, gentlemen, I may be some time"—that Captain Oates, only I changed it so it could be said by a woman.'

'I see.'

'I'm interested in old things, I've got lots of old prints and clothes and things.'

'And politics too,' said Montgomerie.

He drove her home. It was pretty much as he expected. Sort of Bohemian with the persistent odour of joss-sticks. He sat in an old armchair and she gave him weak tea with no milk, though he could have sugar if he wished. He wasn't upset by the hammer and sickle poster on the wall, she'd grow out of that; it was the pot of left-over lentil soup which could be heated if he was hungry, and it was the offer of a dinner of cauliflower cheese if he'd care to come round about seven, but no wine, because they crush grapes to make that.

As he drove back to his flat he thought it odd that he could fall in and out of love in such a short space of time.

CHAPTER 6

Monday, October 14, 9.00 a.m.
The wind sliced keenly off the sea, the clouds rolled in from Northern Ireland, grey, slow, and heavy. Sussock shivered. He was wearing a heavy coat, two pairs of socks, hiking boots, thick trousers, a warm hat and still he shivered. Before him he could see the expanse of the beach north of Machrihanish stretching into the distance. Behind the beach were the sand dunes, some thirty to thirty-five feet high, topped with Marram grass.

'It's nice in the summer,' said the man standing beside him. His name was Angus Stannah, he was a detective-inspector with the Campbeltown Police. He was small and thin for a cop.

'Really, sir.' Sussock reached up and grabbed the brim of his hat as a strong gust of wind reached them.

'Aye,' replied Angus Stannah. 'We get a few visitors too. You know, I can't understand why people should go to Blackpool or Bournemouth with their crowded beaches, when you can walk for miles on our beaches and not meet another living soul.'

'I can't understand it myself, sir,' Sussock replied with sincerity. Crowded beaches, like football matches and smoke-filled railway carriages, were on his list of places to avoid.

Behind Sussock stood DC Bell and behind Stannah stood six uniformed officers and a sergeant from the Campbeltown Police. Behind them stood three cars and a dog van in which the party had that morning travelled from Campbeltown. One of the uniformed officers held an Alsatian on a leash, two others carried spades.

'Well,' said Sussock, 'I suppose we'd better get this show

on the road.' He took his notebook from his inside pocket and thumbed through the pages. 'Ah, yes,' he mumbled. 'Here we are.' Then, louder: 'Yesterday I telephoned the forensic scientist who alerted us to the presence of the Sea Cabbage in the getaway car and I asked her for its precise location. The location of the plant, that is. She said it was on the crest of a dune, half a mile north of Machrihanish. Apparently a group of botanists placed a large rock about eighteen inches high, which they also painted white, near the colony of Sea Cabbage as a sort of marker for their future reference.'

'So all we have to do is look for a white stone and then slip the dog.'

'That's about it,' agreed Sussock.

'I'll lead,' said Stannah, 'we'll walk along the golf-course and then out on to the dunes, don't be tempted to drop down on to the beach, you two gentlemen from Glasgow, or you'll have a devil of a job getting back up.'

Stannah walked away from the cars, northwards on to the golf-course and the others followed, falling into a single file. Sussock found it a hard slog going across the fairway, and when the party reached the dunes his feet slipped sideways in the sand, despite the tread on the sole of his boots, and his calves began to ache. Eventually Stannah led the way on to a path which had been worn in to the vegetation. It was soft and springy to walk on; nevertheless it took the party twenty minutes to cover the half mile.

Stannah stopped and turned to look behind him, back towards Machrihanish, a few cottages, a pub, the golf-club house, a shop or two, a large hotel which had been boarded up. 'This, I think,' he said, 'is about half a mile from Machrihanish.'

'I think you're right,' said Sussock.

'Well, we're behind the dune.' Stannah turned again, looking to his left, to the west. 'If we walk up to the west we can start seeking out the white-painted rock.' He started to walk up through the Marram grass to the top of the dune, beyond which lay a steep drop to the beach. Sussock and the others followed.

'Look for a white-painted rock,' yelled Stannah, and the sergeant repeated the instruction.

Then DC Bell said, in a voice which irritated Sussock by its lack of enthusiasm, "There it is.'

Sussock followed Bell's outstretched hand. 'Yes,' he said, 'that's got to be it.'

The rock was oval in shape, about a foot from end to end and had been lavishly coated with white paint.

'Can't see anything here which looks like cabbage,' said Stannah. 'Marram grass, herbs, a few flowers.'

'Fortunately or unfortunately, depending on your point of view, we're not looking for cabbage,' Sussock replied. He was looking to the north, out to sea. He fancied he could make out Gigha on the horizon.

'Handler!' Stannah called to the police officer who held the dog. 'Bring your dog here, please, and slip the leash when we're out of the way.'

The handler held the eager Alsatian by the collar and walked her up to the small white-painted rock. The rest of the party retreated back down the dune to the path. The handler knelt down by the side of the dog and patted her side. Then he slipped the leash.

From the pathway, Sussock and the others watched the nimble animal weave about the clumps of Marram grass with her nose to the ground. Within three minutes of being released by the handler, the dog had found a small pocket of sand among the vegetation and stood on it, pawing and barking. The handler ran forward and fastened the leash on the dog's neck. He patted her before leading her away.

'All right,' said Stannah. 'Start digging.' The two men who carried the spades advanced up to the west of the dune and started to shovel away the sand where the dog had stood barking. Presently the two officers stopped digging and looked down into the hole that had been excavated. One, not surprisingly the younger of the two, turned and managed to walk some distance into a thick stand of Marram before throwing up.

'Looks like they've found her,' said Bell and started to walk forward.

'We'll wait for the report, laddie,' said Stannah. Bell halted in his tracks.

The remaining officer drove his spade into the ground and walked towards Sussock, Stannah and Bell.

'Human remains, sir,' he said, addressing Stannah. 'About eighteen inches down. Badly decomposed.'

'Thank you, laddie,' said Stannah.

Sussock liked the composure of the young officer.

They were indeed human remains. The grave was short, shallow and narrow. The body had been laid on its side with the legs folded up in front of the chest and the arms crossed above the knees. Mostly it was a skeleton, but there was still an abundance of rotting flesh and an exploded stomach. There was hair on the head which had been turned sideways and upwards so that the teeth grinned from amid the putrefaction.

'Screen,' said Stannah.

Two officers came forward carrying five-foot lengths of wood which they hammered into the ground around the perimeter of the grave. From the staves they suspended a black canvas sheet and pegged it into the ground. Stannah turned to Sussock. 'I suppose you'll be wanting to call in your pathologist now.'

Sussock said 'Yes.'

'I'll leave two men here. We'll wait at the car park. I'll radio for a mobile incident room to be brought out.'

'We might need arc lights if he's delayed in getting here.'

'Aye, we could lay those on.' Then Stannah added, as though he was to be dipping into his own pocket, 'I suppose he'll be wanting a hotel room?'

'The best,' said Sussock.

Dr Reynolds came down that day and arrived in his Volvo estate car just before 4.00 p.m. He was given a room in the same hotel where Sussock and Bell had rooms. Dr Reynolds was given what the bustling manager chose to call the 'executive suite', really just a large room with bathroom and a view over Campbeltown Loch. The tall, silver-haired pathologist declined the offer of a porter and carried his luggage, which included a sinister-looking black bag, up from his car to his hotel room.

He washed and changed and then drove out to Machrihanish, accompanied by Ray Sussock and DI Stannah. They walked along the sand dune to the shallow grave which was hidden behind the flapping canvas screen, arriving just as the light was fading and the constables standing there were handing over duty. Reynolds peered over the top of the screen. 'How long has she been like this?' he asked.

'Probably about two years, sir,' Sussock replied.

'No, I meant how long has the body been exposed?'

'About six or seven hours, sir.'

'Since shortly before you telephoned me?'

'Yes, sir, about half an hour before.'

The pathologist grunted. 'Well, I don't think we need leave her there any longer, she must be getting a bit chilly, don't you think, Sergeant?'

'Well, yes. If you think it should be moved, sir, we . . .' Sussock began to falter. 'You said "she", sir? You can tell it is the body of a female?'

'I'm pretty well certain, Sergeant,' said Renolds, stepping back from the screen.

The corpse was lifted on to a stretcher, covered in a

black shroud and taken in the back of a dark-painted van to the mortuary in the basement of the building in Campbeltown which used to be called the cottage hospital. At dinner that night, Reynolds attacked his lobster voraciously and entertained Sussock and a pale-looking Bell with the case of a body which had been discovered on the salt marsh and had been partly consumed by crabs before it was discovered.

Tuesday, October 15, 9.00 a.m.

A hospital orderly assisted, taking notes as Reynolds dictated, passing instruments as requested by Reynolds. Sussock and Bell were in attendance standing at the side of the room. It was a small room and, given the nature of its use, both Sussock and Bell found it claustrophobic. The centre of the room was taken up by a metal table which was supported by a single central pillar. A tray of surgical instruments stood on a trolley at the side of the table and also on the trolley was the black bag containing Reynolds's instruments. On the table lay the remains of an adult human being. It lay on its side in the manner in which it had been buried, a near foetal position with the head twisted upwards, the exposed jaws and empty eye sockets turned towards the bright lights on the ceiling. The remains were mostly skeletal with scrags of fabric and areas of decaying flesh.

At the side of the room opposite to where Bell and Sussock stood were a series of X-ray prints which hung in front on an illuminated panel.

Reynolds cleared his throat and then said, 'I think we'll begin by trawling for clues as to the identity of the cadaver. The X-rays establish the cause of death as being either gunshot wounds or brain damage following a severe blow to the skull, or both. But we'll come on to that in due course. We have the remains of an adult human, badly decomposed . . .'

The attendant began to take notes.

'The damp dunes would have helped the rate of decomposition. Dry sand would have preserved the body much better.' Reynolds took a tape-measure from the tray and stretched it along the spine of the corpse. 'Spinal length from top to bottom vertebra is . . . thirty-six inches. We usually take the length of the spine to be approximately thirty-five per cent of the body height, which in this case gives us an overall height of five and a half feet. That's an approximation,' he said, turning to the two policemen.

Sussock nodded.

'Sex, now. Well, we have a vertical forehead, rounded orbits in the skull and a wide and squat pelvic structure. The first indications are that these are female remains.'

The pathologist turned, took a long-bladed scalpel from the tray and forced his hands along the rigid thighs of the corpse towards the midriff. He peeled away a layer of cloth and plunged the scalpel into the jellied remains.

'What I'm looking for,' he said, inclining his head to look down his arms at his hands, 'is for any sign of the uterus. The prostate in the male and the uterus in the female, they are what procreation is all about and both organs are among the most resistant to putrefaction. Very handy for determining sex. But in this case, I'm afraid she's too far gone. There's something mushy in there, but I can't identify it. But it's no great loss.' He pulled his hands away from the body. 'I'm certain from the pelvic structure and the shape of the skull that this is the corpse of a female. Another, non-medical, indication is this here, it appears to have been a wedding-ring on the appropriate finger. Men wear wedding-rings, of course, but not so commonly as women.'

The attendant made a note on his pad.

'There are one or two scraps of clothing which are not too far gone, they might be identifiable. Jar, please.'

The attendant handed a circular glass jar to Reynolds, who peeled away a piece of fabric from the corpse and dropped it in the jar. The attendant sealed the jar and attached a label to it.

'You can take that back to Glasgow,' said Reynolds, 'the forensic science team should be able to identify the fabric. To my untrained eye it looks like a piece of denim. Right, age now.' Reynolds turned his attention to the skull. 'This can be the most difficult bit,' he said, not looking at anyone in particular. 'It's always dodgy assessing the age from skeleton remains in the case of an adult. The most we can hope for is to make a guess which could be up to ten years wide of the mark. The sutures in the skull are just beginning to knit, so an approximation of the age could be, say, thirty-five. But, she could be as young as twenty-five or as old as forty-five.

'Positive identification will have to be made using dental records. I'll take the jaws out of the skull and take them to the School of Dentistry in Glasgow. I gather you suspect the identity of this woman, Sergeant?'

'Yes, sir,' said Sussock, 'we do.'

'Good, then it should be a simple matter for you to obtain a warrant to enable the School of Dentistry to gain access to her dental records. They should be able to match the teeth with her records. If they do have a positive identification you're home and dry. If they don't you have a problem.'

'We're reasonably certain we know the identity, sir,' Sussock replied.

'Good. I hope you're right for your sakes,' said Reynolds, 'otherwise you've got a lot of work to do. Now would you like to come and look at the X-rays?' He walked over to the X-ray transparencies. Sussock and Bell joined him, both walking round the foot of the table, rather than the head, although to walk round the top would have been a shorter route. Reynolds took a pen from his pocket and outlined the image on the first plate.

'The skull, gentlemen,' said the pathologist. 'Note the fracture here.' He tapped the pencil against the plate. 'That fracture is just above and behind the left ear and in itself would have been powerful enough to cause death. It would cause severe damage to the brain.'

'What sort of implement would have been used?' asked Sussock.

'Well, I would have said something that has a sharp point, but here—' he ran the pen along the edge of the fracture—'here is an indication that the implement had a linear quality.'

'So the sharp corner of something long caused this?'

'Probably.'

'The end of a stave, wielded not jabbed, for example.'

'That sort of thing,' nodded Reynolds. 'Now whether this blow did cause death or not I can't tell, because she was also shot. You see on these plates here—' Reynolds edged towards two other plates—'these little white dots here and here, and also here, these are pellets from a shot-gun cartridge, twelve-bore I should think, judging by their size.'

'Now the peculiar thing is that there appear to be two definite clusters, one about her midriff and the other about her knees.'

'She was shot twice,' said Sussock. 'Once in the body and once in the legs.'

'That's what I thought at first,' Reynolds nodded in agreement. 'But now I don't think so. You see, there don't seem to be enough pellets for two twelve-bore cartridges. I think she was shot only once.'

Bell asked, 'Why are the pellets so far apart?'

'That is the problem,' said Reynolds. 'I think there are two possible answers. The first is that she was shot from a distance of about fifty yards, so some of the pellets would have missed her, you know passed either side of her. But the X-rays indicate that she has absorbed all the pellets from the cartridge. The second flaw in the theory of her being shot at a distance is that the pellets seem to be too deeply embedded. So I would reject the theory that she was shot at a distance. The theory I do favour is that she was shot when she had assumed a position which brought her knees close to her chest. A posture which is similar to the way she is lying now.'

'You mean curled up in bed,' said Sussock.

'Or kneeling,' said Bell.

Reynolds smiled at him. 'Yes, that would be my guess. You see this pellet here—' he tapped the X-ray transparency. 'It does not lie very deeply beneath the surface of the skin, which has not decayed very much, but it is about six inches above the knee. If she was standing when shot we could expect this pellet to have penetrated much deeper than this. If we assume, as DC Bell suggests, that she was kneeling, facing the gun, then the pellet will have entered just above her knee and driven up her leg to the point here where it came to rest. Like I said, the pellet is close to the surface of the skin, but, if the theory is correct, then it represents a wound which is six inches deep. The decomposition of the body has obviously disturbed the pellets, but we can hazard a guess at the manner in which she was shot, kneeling, facing the gun, at a distance of about ten feet. And because she was kneeling, the blow to her head was sustained after she was shot.'

'So it was murder,' said Sussock.

'Well, that's for you to say, Sergeant,' said Reynolds. 'All I can say is that you can discount suicide. The gun was too far away, apart from the fact that suicide victims don't bury themselves. An accident? Improbable, I'd say. Her body would have been flung backwards by the blast, but I doubt that there would have been sufficient force to damage her skull in the manner it has been damaged, and any damage to the skull would have been sustained at the back, not the side. Also, I don't think that people who are shot accidentally are usually kneeling and facing a gun which seems to have been held at normal shoulder height, judging by the direction of travel of this pellet, the one which entered her above the knee. This seems to me to be like a person adopting a posture of submission, maybe pleading for her life. But that's conjecture.'

'The blow to the head,' said Sussock. 'Could it have been caused by being struck on the head by the stock of the shot-gun?'

'Most certainly,' agreed Reynolds. 'That would indeed be consistent with the injury sustained.'

'So she's shot and then cracked across the head with the stock of the gun,' said Sussock, more to himself than anyone else. 'Odd thing to do—blast her, then clobber her.'

'We can't tell exactly what happened,' said Reynolds. 'There could have been a time gap of about fifteen or twenty minutes between these injuries. It's possible he thought he had killed her—I'm using the masculine here for convenience—she may have lost consciousness after being shot and then come round and started screaming with pain, so he panicked, picked up the gun and wham! Used it like a club.' Reynolds returned to the table in the centre of the room. 'Obliging of her to have turned her head this way,' he said, 'makes my job easier.' He began to prise open the jaws.

'Indeed, sir,' said Sussock as he and Bell returned to their former position at the side of the room. He winced inwardly as the jaws made a creaking sound as they were forced open.

'Stiff, stiff,' said Reynolds to himself. Then to the assistant: 'Have a polythene bag ready, please, one of the medium-sized ones.' Reynolds turned again to the corpse. 'What I'm going to do is to clear away what flesh remains and cut away what's left of her tendons on both sides of the jaw.' He started cutting and scraping and then replaced the instrument he was using in a tray filled with disinfectant. 'Now, just to get hold correctly and I should be able to disarticulate the jaw . . .'

Sussock was relieved that the corpse was obscured from view by Dr Reynolds. The description of what was happening together with the sound as the pathologist removed the jaw from the corpse was enough for him. It was evidently too much for Bell, who excused himself and left the laboratory.

Eventually Dr Reynolds held up the jaw for Sussock's edification and then dropped it into a polythene bag. The attendant sealed the bag and labelled it. The pathologist moved away from the body and Sussock saw the body with just the upper set of teeth left in place to smile at the ceiling.

'I'll take the jaw up to the School of Dentistry today, Sergeant,' said Reynolds. 'We have to put it in cold storage as soon as possible. I think the lower set of teeth should be sufficient to ascertain her identity, she has had a lot of work done, filling in nearly every molar and a crown by the look of it. I don't think it's necessary to take the top teeth out. So I'll leave them. It's a messy business anyway, involving sawing through the skull.'

'If you think that's sufficient, sir,' said Sussock, who for himself felt it was all quite enough for one day.

'I'm sure it will be,' said Reynolds, peeling off his surgical gloves. 'Well, I think that's me. Spot of lunch and then drive to Glasgow. The School of Dentistry won't be able to do a thing unless you get a warrant authorizing her dentist to release her records. Once that's done, it's only a five-minute job to match the jaws with the records. Join me for lunch, Sergeant?'

'That's kind of you, sir,' said Sussock. 'But I don't have much of an appetite.'

*

Outside the hospital Sussock saw Bell stepping out of a telephone kiosk. Bell approached him.

'Who were you 'phoning?' Sussock demanded as Bell drew near. Sussock noticed Bell pale, then blush.

'What? Oh, only home, Sarge,' Bell stammered, 'just putting a call through to home.'

'You went out to get air, not attend to your private affairs.'

'I know, Sarge, I just thought I might take the opportunity . . .'

'In future 'phone your family when you're off duty.'

'Sarge.'

'However, since you obviously feel like telephoning, you can go to the Police Station and telephone Inspector Donoghue. Ask him if he'll be so good as to obtain a warrant to permit Flora Middleton's dentist to release her dental records to the School of Dentistry. You can add that Dr Reynolds is delivering the lower jaw of the body found in the sand dune direct to the School this afternoon. Also inform the Inspector that we will be returning to Glasgow this afternoon.'

'Very good, sir,' replied Bell with a curtness which annoyed Sussock.

'Join me at the hotel,' said Sussock sharply.

In the old house a man put down the telephone and went to the second room where the other men and the women sat by the log fire.

'He wants a drink,' said the first man.

'No.' The big man shook his head. 'We agreed. No share-outs until the heat's off.'

'He's desperate.'

'Why?'

'He's got money problems.'

'Who hasn't?'

'Some guy has got the squeeze on him.'

'Who?'

'Some overgrown ned called Wee Timmy the Rat. Operates as a moneylender.'

'I don't like moneylenders,' said the big man. 'No, I don't like them at all.'

'He's into him for four grand.'

'Four grand!'

'How much did he borrow?'

'Five hundred.'

'So why the big squeeze?'

'He didn't say, but I can guess one reason: Wee Timmy the Rat's in for a drink himself.'

'He knows we pulled the Post Office job?' The big man put his can of lager down. The woman sitting next to him looked frightened. The man's eyes hardened.

'How? How does he know?'

'I don't know, boss, I'm just guessing, but loan sharks squeeze for what they can get. He would reckon he could squeeze for four grand if he had a hand in something big, like a quarter of a million snatch.'

'This guy's dangerous.'

'Wee Timmy the Rat, you mean?'

'Aye,' said the big man. 'This is a one-job outfit. When we share out we split and we don't meet up again. That was agreed. But while we're together we're tight. It's got to be like that, otherwise there's chinks in the armour. One of us is in trouble so we help him out.'

'You're not going to give him the bread?'

'Am I hell! No, we pay a call tonight, late. Then we go and see this guy they call Wee Timmy the Rat.'

'All of us?'

'No, me, Seaweed here, and Bonzer. The rest stay, that includes you, Whannell.'

'OK.' Whannell nodded, but he didn't look pleased.

'I think he's got drogues, Wee Timmy the Rat.'

'He's small meat. Remember who we are, Bunny. Top team, put together for one job. Top team, right?'

'Right,' said Bunny. Then he went back to finish his shift by the 'phone which stood by the window which looked out into the farmyard, down the long drive and on to the main road.

CHAPTER 7

Tuesday, October 15, 8.30 p.m.

'You shouldn't have come here,' said Bell. 'It's too dangerous.' He shut the door rapidly behind them.

'We took care.' The big man lumbered down the hallway. 'Nobody saw us.'

'Come through and keep your voice down.' Bell led the three men into the sitting-room of his flat.

'Who made this mess?' The big man sat in an armchair.

'Wee Timmy the Rat,' said Bell. 'His drogues anyway. He too sat down, looking weary. 'I just need four grand to pay him off. Then I won't have any more hassle. I reckon I've got at least fifty thousand coming from the job, you could let me have four.'

'No deal,' said the big man. 'We agreed. No share-out until the Bill has other worries and has forgotten about us.'

'But the notes are not traceable, Izzy.' Bell raised his head and looked at the big man. 'That's why we hit the Post Office; they use the old notes for welfare handouts, Izzy, for God's sake.'

'We made an agreement. Anyway, how did this little moneylender know you were in on the Post Office job?' Bell remained silent. Confessing wouldn't repair the damage, so eventually he said, 'Beats me, Izzy.'

'We'll get it out of the bastard,' said the big man. 'Won't we, Bunny?'

Bunny started to grin.

'Seaweed?'

'Certainly will, Izzy.'

'He won't be bothering you again, Matthew. He's just one of a number of little problems you can turn your back on, because you're in the money now.' Seaweed, standing by the smashed television, said, 'That's right, Matthew, you can gamble it all.'

Bell glared at him. 'That's not funny.'

'You bet it's not, toe-rag. It was your gambling got this moneylender in on our act.'

'How did you know that?'

'Inspired guess, cop. Couldn't trust you. Once a cop always a cop.'

'That true, Matthew?' asked Izzy, dangerously cool.

'What if it is?'

'It was silly, Matthew,' said Izzy.

'So I have a problem, don't we all? Look, you've got a lot to thank me for, I put this team together, didn't I? Best men on police files, I brought you together for the one job. Top team, remember, that's what we said. Top team.'

'OK, let's stop arguing already,' said Izzy. 'This Little Timmy the Rat, where does he hang out?'

'I have his address. I wrote it down in my book here.' Bell winced as he reached forward to take the notebook from the low table.

'You OK?'

'Yes.' Bell sat back in the chair. 'His drogues worked me over a couple of days ago. Careful if you meet them. They're heavy.'

'Not too heavy for us,' said Izzy the big man.

'What are you going to do?' Bell copied the address on to a scrap of paper and handed it to Izzy.

'Do? Do, my child?' said Izzy in an affected manner. 'We are going to pay a parochial visit on this poor sinner, and we is going to chastise the devil from him, brother.'

'He's a front man,' said Bell. 'He lives with his old mother, a real thin-lipped witch. She's the brains. You'll find the float in their house, about twenty thousand pounds, ready cash for their operation. If you lift that you'll stop the operation. If you run into the heavies, tell them you're suspending the operation and you might avoid aggro. The heavies are not hired, they're working off a debt.'

'Got it all worked out, hasn't he? This address, it's not far from here?'

Bell shook his head. 'Just up Maryhill Road. You can walk from here.'

The big man started to turn.

'Izzy,' said Bell.

The big man turned back and faced Bell, who sat motionless in the chair and stared at the floor.

'Izzy,' he said. 'We have a problem.'

'What now?'

'I was in Campbeltown this morning, me and another CID officer, old guy by the name of Sussock. We attended the post-mortem of Middleton's wife.'

Izzy paused. Then, with an edge to his voice, he said, 'So?'

'So Whannell dumped the body, didn't he?'

'Our Whannell, the wheelman?'

'The one and the same.'

'Again, so?' But the edge on his voice was harder.

'Middleton recommended him. I approached him, he seemed OK. Reckoned he could get a car. Which he did, in a way.'

'What do you mean?'

'I mean he knocked off Middleton's old car, didn't he? And it wasn't coincidence, the clown kept track of it after

Middleton sold it. He must have had a duplicate set of keys.'

'The idiot.'

'The law knows it's him. They have a record of him smashing the car after he dumped the body. He was drunk.'

'That's what you meant when you said they were on to the car?'

'That's right.'

'Matthew,' said Izzy with a note of barely restrained anger, 'I think you had better tell us what the Bill knows. See if we can rescue anything and stay cool, see if we have to run like now.'

'OK, OK.' Bell held up his hand, paused and then said, 'They know Middleton's wife was murdered. They know Whannell used Middleton's car to dump the body. When I signed off duty this afternoon they hadn't positively identified the body, but they will, they may already have done, because Middleton told me what he did to his wife, he shot her. That was when he recommended Whannell.'

'Some recommendation.'

'No, he was good, Whannell, he did well. He drove well on the job. He disposed of the body of Middleton's wife alone, and he didn't start blabbering when the Campbeltown cops felt his collar for drunken driving. But he goes and ruins it all by knocking off Middleton's old car.'

'So the filth have a link between Middleton's murdered wife and the raid on the Post Office run by Middleton.'

'That's about it,' said Bell.

'So how long have we got, Matthew?'

'We'll likely be calling on Middleton tomorrow. Like, about seven in the morning. We're already looking for Whannell.'

'We?' said Seaweed.

'They!' said Bell. 'They, they, they.' He rested his

forehead in his hands. 'Christ, what a mess, Izzy, what a mess.'

'You said it,' said the big man. 'Middleton thought up the job, you put it together, now it's you and Middleton that's blowing the whole works. How strong is Middleton?'

'You know him as well as I do.'

'You know him socially. You know him better.'

'I'd hardly call GA socializing.'

'So is he strong or is he strong?'

'He's weak. Sussock's already interviewed him. I've seen Sussock's recording. He's convinced that Middleton is hiding something. He'll not stand up to intensive questioning.'

'So what do we do, bright boy?'

'I don't know!' yelled Bell.

'We have to rub him out, perhaps,' said Izzy quietly. There was a heavy silence in the room.

'I don't know, Izzy.' Bell shook his head slowly. 'I mean, that's murder, Izzy.'

'Sure it's murder. But how else are we going to stop him talking? Anyway he murdered his wife, didn't he, so it'll be rough justice.'

'Yes, he knocked her off all right,' admitted Bell. 'Wanted her life insurance to pay off gambling debts.'

'Was he going to make it look like an accident?'

'I think so. I don't know the details. Chrissake! It didn't go to plan anyway and he ended up blowing her in half and burying her on the Mull of Kintyre and still hoped for the insurance even then; people who remain missing for so many years are assumed to be dead. Still he was desperate, he did a desperate thing.'

'You're telling me.' Izzy took out a packet of cigarettes and lit one. 'So what are we going to do about Middleton? He's landed us in a stooshie.'

'Maybe we should go and lean on him a little, Izzy,' said Seaweed, himself leaning against the wall.

'Couldn't we spirit him away?' said Bell. 'Give him his share, his passport, and put him on a plane someplace.'

'That really would make the filth smell a rat,' said Izzy.

'Oh, they smell one already.' Bell sat back in the chair. 'They smell a whole nest of them. Look, what's the difference? We either bump him off or send him airmail. Either way the law's going to be suspicious.'

'OK, but we have to send him where he'll do least damage,' said Izzy. 'How long will he survive abroad? He'll only be taking his fifty thousand, and most of that will go on buying silence. He's got no connections abroad, he's got no connections here, he's a one job merchant, useful for inside information only. He's redundant, Matthew, he'll last a year at the most. Me, I'm going to Spain, I have a villa in Marbella and a few mates. I'll lie low for a couple of years, then I'll come back and put another job together. Middleton can't do that. He'll surface too quickly and then he'll start shooting his mouth off.'

'So what do you suggest?'

'He's got to be snuffed out. We have to send him to the one place he can't do any damage.'

'Drastic, Izzy.'

'We could make it look like an accident.'

'How?'

'I don't know exactly. We'll work something out.'

'Well, I tell you, my friend . . .'

'I'm not your friend, Matthew.'

'All right. It's nine o'clock now, we have little Timmy the Rat to deal with and Middleton, all in the space of less than ten hours. That is before I call on Middleton in an official capacity. But maybe I'd better stay here, it would be too risky if I went.'

'It would be too risky if you didn't, Matthew. Do you have any handcuffs here, or rope?'

'Handcuffs, yes,' said Bell.

'Good.' Izzy smiled. 'That's good.'

Half an hour later Izzy, Seaweed and Bunny stood outside the door of Wee Timmy the Rat's flat. Izzy knocked on the door. It was opened by the young man who tried to shut it again. At the same time Matthew Bell left his car and walked up the drive to the door of Middleton's bungalow in Bearsden. He pressed the door buzzer.

'You shouldn't have come,' said Middleton.

'We have a problem.' Bell spoke flatly. 'You'd better let me in.'

'What is it? Are they on to us?'

Bell pushed past Middleton. Middleton shut the door.

'Good as,' said Bell. 'You'll be getting a visit from the old sergeant tomorrow. We dug up the body of your wife this morning.'

Middleton said, 'Oh my God.' He went into his sitting-room. Bell followed. Middleton went across to the drinks cabinet and took a slug of scotch straight from the bottle, but it didn't stop his hands shaking. He sank into a chair and said, 'Oh God, oh God, oh God. Matthew, what are we going to do?' He looked up at Bell with big pleading eyes. 'Matthew, what am I going to do, how did they get on to me?'

'The car,' said Bell. He went across to the drinks cabinet and looked at the contents. 'Don't you have any beer?'

'What! Christ, no, just what you see. What do you mean, the car?'

'Whannell, you know Whannell, subject of your glowing recommendation. He nicked your old motor, your old Ford.'

'I sold it a year ago.'

'Well, Whannell went and liberated it back, didn't he? Went all the way in to England to pinch it, the new owner apparently having moved to Carlisle in the interim.' Bell poured himself a gin. He was beginning to feel a little more confident, but he went careful on the alcohol. Couldn't afford to over do it, not tonight.

'He didn't!'

'Oh, but he did. Says a lot for Whannell that he kept tabs on it over that distance. Quick re-spray and a nip up the M74 for the Post Office job.' Bell sipped the drink. He felt a growing sense of power, he was finding it not an unpleasant sensation. Tonight, for one night, I am Death, the destroyer of things. 'It might have been all right but the trouble is that when he used the car to dispose of the corpse of the good Mrs Middleton he did a couple of stupid things. He bureid her next to some rare plant, only one colony of it in Scotland, and he has to carry a bit of it back in the car, which remains in the car wedged between the seat and the side panel these two years. Then he went and had a skinful while he's burying her and smashed the car in the Campbeltown area on the weekend of your wife's disappearance. Nothing to connect the two at the time, but when the same car is used in the Post Office raid, a Post Office managed by yourself, well, a moron with a glass eye can see the connection. They go over your old car with a toothcomb and find a bit of this plant, hey, we took the dog to the area round the plant this morning and released her and, before you could have finished a cigarette, she was pawing at the sand dune and barking.' Bell took a sip of the gin. 'You've got about eight hours, Hamish.'

'Me? What about . . .' Middleton looked white, a glazed expression, someone wishing he was a million miles away.

'It just needs a positive ID to be made on your wife's remains and, as you well know, that will be a formality. It's probably already been done, the pathologist brought her jaw up from Campbeltown this afternoon.'

'He did what?'

'He wrenched the jaw from the skull, or rather what remained of it, you should have seen the mess she was in, so that the teeth can be matched against her dental records.'

'Matt, listen, Matt, you've got to tell me what to say, you've got to help me fix up a story. I'm not going to stand up to an interrogation, I'll crack, I'll tell them everything, Matt. See that old cop who called a couple of days ago, I could tell he knew something. I'm scared that I'm going to say too much.'

Bell put the gin down on the sideboard. He said, 'See, Hamish, that's what I've called about.'

It was another hour before Izzy came to Middleton's house. Bell let him in and showed him into the sitting-room where Middleton was lying on the floor, his hands shackled behind him, a handkerchief in his mouth held in place by his tie. There was blood coming from his nose and a couple of legs from the coffee table were smashed.

'Better get all this tidied up to make it look right,' said Izzy. 'Bunny, take this table here and put it in the dustbin out the back.'

Bell stooped and picked up the spilt gin bottle and his glass. 'My glass," he said, 'got my prints all over it. I'll wipe it.'

'Good. I take it our friend didn't care for our idea.'

'Didn't exactly go down a bomb,' said Bell. He took the glass he had used into the kitchen and washed it.

'You'll have no more trouble from the wee moneylender,' said Izzy when Bell returned to the sitting-room. 'We took his float, just in case. Extra twenty thousand for us. Split seven ways if it's all the same to you, Matthew.'

'Sure, sure,' said Bell, a little nervous again. 'Big money all round.'

'Not a bad rate for half an hour's work at that,' Izzy

agreed. 'You won't get no more trouble from his old woman either.'

'You didn't work the old woman over!'

'Bunny tapped her right enough.' Izzy wrapped his hand in a handkerchief and grabbed a bottle of whisky from the drinks cupboard. 'Who'd have thought an old bird in a wheelchair could squeal so much; like a parrot in a cage full of hungry rats. Mind you, I suppose if your one and only was getting rolled in front of you you'd kick up a bit of a fuss. He wasn't a big boy though, was he? Wonder if Seaweed was a bit too rough with him?' This last more to himself than Bell.

'Still, it's done now,' said Bell.

'Aye.'

'And more money all round.'

'Even more when we carve old Hamish's share.' Izzy raised the bottle. 'Cheers, Hamish.'

Middleton squirmed on the floor and tried to speak.

'You didn't tell him?' Izzy asked.

'Not in so many words, but he got the message quick enough, that's how the furniture got smashed. But we made the right decision, he said he'd talk.'

'Oh, he did,' said Izzy. 'Well, that eases my mind.' He looked at Middleton. 'You're going to take a short walk off a high bridge,' Izzy said.

Bell said, 'After it's done, I think I'd better come back to the farm. It's getting dicey for me.'

'No, Matthew.' Izzy eyed him squarely. 'You've got to stay put and help us keep one jump ahead. We'll tell you when you're time's up.'

One hour later Bell staggered back from the bushes to the car.

'That you?' said Izzy. He didn't disguise his anger.

'Aye,' said Bell weakly, leaning against the car.

'Oh, good. Christ, you screw up all round and then

you have to do that.'

'I've never killed anybody before.'

'You did more than kill somebody, young Matthew, you've screwed up, again.'

'It wasn't my fault, you heaved the bastard over while I was trying to get them off him.'

'What did you want us to do, for Christ sake?' Izzy snarled. 'Ask him to stand nice and still, like, while you fixed him so's it would look right.'

'I think I got one off,' Bell said. 'I don't know, perhaps the other . . .'

'That's made it even worse,' said Izzy. 'You're a toe-rag Matthew, you're a walking disaster area. You're a liability.'

'You screwed up, Matthew, cop.' Seaweed's voice floated out from the dimness of the rear seat. 'You screwed up good and proper this time.'

11.00 p.m. King and Abernethy were covering the graveyard shift. They had read each other's newspapers. They had done the crosswords. Outside, it began to rain, pattering against the black window-panes. At the end of the room one filament bulb was flickering madly in its death throes.

Is it always like this?' Abernethy glanced across the desks at King. He looked to King for advice, guidance, leadership. King was twenty-five years old.

'Always,' said King. 'Pass us your paper.'

'You've read it twice.' Abernethy folded his copy of the *Evening Times* and skimmed it towards King.

'Twice? Is that all?' King grinned and unfolded the paper. 'Have you done the crossword yet?'

'You did it an hour ago—before I got to it. Wouldn't mind but it's my paper.'

'Rank has its privileges, my son,' said King. 'Speaking of which, mine is white with no sugar.'

'That'll be right,' said Abernethy.

Then the telephone rang.

'Gentleman called Kyle on the 'phone for you,' said the pedantic Hamilton from the extension on the front desk.

'Kyle?' repeated King.

'Kyle, sir,' said Phil Hamilton, twenty-four years old, and it would seem destined for a slow methodical plod through the uniformed branch, getting ten marks for observation of regulations, no marks for style.

'Did he say what it was about?'

'No, sir, asked for you by name though.'

'Better put him on, then.'

The line clicked a couple of times. King heard Phil Hamilton say, 'Go ahead now, please.'

'Hello there,' said a confident voice.

'Detective-Constable King here.'

'Alan Kyle,' said the voice. 'I've just returned from aboard, business. I'm catching up on correspondence and have just come across your circular in connection with stolen firearms.'

'Yes,' said King snatching his pad and ballpoint. He trapped the telephone receiver between his head and shoulder and made ready to write.

'Well, I think I may be able to shed light on the subject of the missing shot-guns. I don't know anything about the hunting rifle, I don't have a licence to deal in such things . . .'

'You're a gun-dealer, sir?'

'You insult me, sir,' said Kyle. 'I'm an antique-dealer, a reputable one in a trade with more than its fair share of shady characters.'

'Indeed, sir,' replied King. 'You say you have some information.'

'The information I have is, I regret, limited. I think I may have been offered the guns you describe in the circular. Two Purdys, nineteenth-century models. They don't often come our way, especially a brace of them. Nice guns.'

'Did you buy them?'

'I did not. I was suspicious of the man.'

'Did you report it to the police? That is, the attempt to sell you the guns.'

'No.'

'Didn't you see the first circular?'

A pause. Then: 'No, I can't honestly say I did.'

'Well, at least you've given us a lead now.'

'When was the robbery?'

'Six months ago.'

'Then, that absolves me of blame, Detective-Constable,' said Kyle, and King could sense him smiling as he said it. 'I've just started trading.'

'You say you've just returned from abroad: when did you receive the offer of the guns?'

'Just before I left for France. Three weeks ago.'

Kyle lived in a substantial detached house built of grey stone in Clarkston. Upon the ring of his doorbell, Kyle was heard striding down the hallway with a heavy footfall. He flung the door wide and stood there, a tall man with a neat silver beard. He insisted on shaking hands before stepping aside to let the two officers enter his house. There was something forced and over-confident about his man-of-the-house behaviour which both King and Abernethy found unsettling.

'Alone at home,' said Kyle as he shut the door behind the two cops. 'Er, the wife's away.'

'I see,' said King.

The hallway of Kyle's house was piled high with tables, wardrobes, chairs and there was a narrow passage between the furniture which led towards the rear of the house.

'Lack of storage space in the shop,' said Kyle, leading

King and Abernethy down the passage. 'All this is French, immediate post-war. Not yet in vogue, but that's the secret of antique-dealing, you have to anticipate what period is going to be in fashion and then buy it up before it gets trendy. Buy while it's still junk being chopped up for firewood and sell it when it becomes antique.'

'Then you sell at a vast profit?' said King, turning sideways to get between two sideboards.

'Yes,' Kyle agreed simply. 'Profit margins of two or three thousand per cent are not unknown in this business.'

At the end of the valley of table tops and chair legs was a door to the right. Kyle opened the door and showed King and Abernethy into the drawing-room of the house. Neat, functional, done in pastel shades, but lacking a woman's touch.

'Drink, gentlemen?'

Both cops declined.

'Oh, come now, gentlemen, accept Scottish hospitality as a Scot. You'll take a dram?'

'No,' said Abernethy. 'Thank you.'

'Not on duty,' said King.

'Aye, well,' said Kyle. 'You'll not object if I have a wee one myself.' He walked to an old table on which stood half a dozen bottles, poured a generous hit of whisky into a glass and drank it neat. 'Take a seat, gentlemen.' King and Abernethy sat together on the settee. King noticed that the fire grate was empty and it suddenly struck him just how cold the house was.

'Sure I can't get you something?' chuffed Kyle, rising up and down on his toes, heavy grey flannels, blue jersey, cravat, and, King thought, thermal underwear too no doubt.

'Let's talk about shot-guns,' said King. He actually saw a wisp of his breath condense in the air. He wondered i

Kyle's offer of a drink would stretch to a mug of hot Bovril.

'Ah yes. Chap came into the shop. Bold as brass.'

'Which is where?'

'St George's. Bottom of the Great Western Road.'

'I haven't noticed it.'

'Like I said, I've just started trading,' said Kyle. 'But it's there all right. Anyway, about three weeks ago, this type came in.'

'Type?'

'Yes, a type. You know—a type.'

'Can you please tell me what you mean by a "type"?'

'Heavens.' Kyle took a sizeable slug of his whisky. 'Scruffy, needed a wash. Combat jacket, jeans, I mean at his age. Not the sort of customer I wish to encourage.'

'Combat jacket?'

'Yes, Mr King, a combat jacket.'

'I'm sorry, please carry on.'

'I thank you, sir.' Kyle gave a supercilious nod. 'Yes, this type. He brought his guns into the shop, complete with presentation case, in which they were carried in a dismantled state.'

'He offered them for sale?'

'Yes, he was anxious for money. He would have taken almost anything I offered. Dare say I turned down a gift.'

'You turned down stolen property. You would have lost your money as well as being done for re-set.'

'Not unless I moved them quickly enough.' He drained his glass.

'Would you recognize this man again?'

'Perhaps.'

'Only perhaps?'

'It's an honest answer.'

King plunged his hand inside his inner coat pocket. 'I have here two photographs, sir, I'd like you to look at them if you'd be so kind. One is a print of a photofit and the other is a photograph taken of a man on his admission to prison. It is a few years old so you'll have to allow for ageing.'

'Allowing for ageing is my business, Mr King.' Kyle took the prints. He held them close and then held them at arm's length. Then he held them close again. Finally he inclined them towards the light. 'It isn't this chap.' He handed the photofit to King, but retained the photograph. 'It could be this type. Would he have grown a beard?'

'He could well have done.'

'A big bushy red beard?'

'A distinct possibility,' conceded King.

'In that case it could be him.'

'Can you remember anything about what was said or anything about him which could help us locate him?' Kyle was silent. Then he said, 'He seemed to live on a farm.'

'A farm!'

'Yes, Mr King, a farm.'

'What makes you say that?'

'Well, he had muddy Wellington boots. I had to clean the floor after he had gone. He smelled like a farmer, sort of earthy. I saw him drive away in a grey Bedford pick-up with the name of some farm written on the outside. The pick-up was empty.'

'Anything else written on the side of the pick-up?'

'Ayrshire,' said Kyle. 'Then a 'phone number. But that I do not recall.'

'Where's Whannell?' said the big man.

'What?' the other man murmured drowsily. 'Oh, it's yourself, Izzy.'

'Aye, it's me. Where's Whannell?'

'Is he not in his bed?' The second man levered himself up on to his elbows.

'Jesus Christ!' said the big man.

CHAPTER 8

Wednesday, October 16, 9.00 a.m.

Donoghue pulled on his pipe and leaned back in his chair. He read King's report of the interview with Kyle and then re-read it. Just as he was completing the second reading there was a sharp tap on the door of his office. He put the report on his desk and said, 'Come in.' Ray Sussock entered Donoghue's office. He was smiling, but he couldn't hide the tiredness brought on by too many years at the coal face; the furrowed brow, the bags under the eyes, the sunken cheeks and the greying hair.

'Something good, Ray?' asked Donoghue.

'Yes, sir.' Ray Sussock handed Donoghue a sheet of paper which was headed 'The Glasgow School of Dentistry'. 'It tells us what we thought all along, but it's confirmation none the less.'

Donoghue took the report from Sussock and read it. 'Take a seat, Ray,' he said when he was still half way through the report. 'I'm not one to have people standing at my desk.'

Sussock sat down. He watched Donoghue read the report. Donoghue wore an intense expression, looking younger than his forty-one years. Sussock noticed that, as always, the Detective-Inspector was immaculately turned out, his jacket and coat hanging on a stand behind his desk, his waistcoat buttoned up with his gold hunter's chain looping across the front. Donoghue put the report down and patted it with a well-manicured hand. 'So,' he said, 'the missing person file on Flora Middleton is closed and a murder file is opened. With who as the prime suspect?'

'Her husband, I would say, sir,' said Sussock.

'I would say so too, Ray. Better go and have a word with him.'

'Not bring him in for questioning?'

'Well, it's up to you, Ray. This is your pigeon.'

'Thank you.'

'Who will you be taking with you?'

'Bell, I guess.'

'You don't sound too enthusiastic. How is he shaping up?'

'Frankly, I don't know.'

'What does that mean, Ray? Don't be afraid to hang out your dirty linen.'

'He doesn't seem to be too interested. No evident enthusiasm. Yesterday, for instance, in Campbeltown, he left the post-mortem, turned his stomach I expect, left to get some air and I found him outside just having made a personal 'phone call. I mean, it's hardly a breach of regulations, but there was something that I didn't like about it. I mean, if he had recovered enough to 'phone his family, he had recovered enough to attend to his duty, even if it was waiting outside the post-mortem clinic to be on hand in case he was needed.'

'That's what he said, is it?' asked Donoghue. 'That he was 'phoning his family?'

'Yes, why?'

'He hasn't got a family. He transferred from the Lothian and Borders Police following his divorce. No children. He could have meant that he was talking to a brother or a sister, or his parents, but he's hardly likely to refer to them as his family.'

'He's not, is he.' Sussock nodded.

'Puzzling,' said Donoghue. 'But don't read too much into it, Ray. We won't sling any mud. Now on to a more encouraging topic, just to keep you informed, especially because I'll be taking the afternoon off so you'll be running the show. Richard King had a response from his circular to all antique shops and gunsmiths. A chap who owns an antique shop in St George's was approached by a fellow trying to unload two Purdys in a presentation case.'

'Was he now.'

'He was indeed. Only three weeks ago to boot. We don't want to assume too much, but it might be the fellow who burgled the stately pile in Perthshire, or whatever it's called now, the old names tend to stick even after all these years.'

'The castle was in the Tayside Region,' said Sussock.

'Well, to continue, if this fellow has been unable to move the guns via reputable dealers, then he must now be resorting to moving them in the underworld.'

'It would make sense. So the boys who robbed the Post Office bought the job lot just for the hunting rifle and one of their gang has taken to doing a bit of moonlighting on his own.'

'The point is that the antique-dealer remembers the man who offered him the guns drove off in a pick-up on which was painted the name of a farm in Ayrshire. He doesn't recall the name of the farm, that would be too much to hope for, but it indicates that the gang may be in a safe house in that area.'

'A farm, you mean?'

'Well, yes.'

'Thin straw.' Sussock shifted on his chair. 'I mean, there's no proof that the hunting rifle which was stolen from the castle near Perth is the same rifle that was pointed at the driver of the armoured vehicle outside the Post Office a week ago tomorrow.'

'There is not,' agreed Donoghue. 'None, save for a point I haven't yet told you. The foregoing was to keep you abreast of developments in the robbery case; the following is for your edification in respect of the Flora Middleton murder. The antique-dealer recognized the photograph of Whannell as being the man who attempted to sell the shot-guns to him.'

'Whannell,' said Sussock, smiling. 'That's a name that keeps cropping up. How did King get hold of the photograph?'

'He plundered your file on Flora Middleton.'

'Did he?'

'Don't get annoyed. You were not around to ask and he knew of the Whannell connection through the car. He makes it his business to keep himself abreast of developments, does young Mr King. He often surprises me with what he knows.'

'So the indication is that the rifle used in the hold-up is the one which was stolen from the castle a few months ago.'

'Yes, if Whannell is involved.'

'Even so, we're not much further forward.'

'Don't get pessimistic, Ray. We know we are not sniffing down the wrong trail with regard to the guns, and it means you can pursue your hunt for Whannell with renewed vigour, in fact you can team up with King and Abernethy. They will be back on duty at two p.m.'

'Can't think where to move from here. Whannell's moved around the bed-sits and shady digs so much that I've lost track. In fact I didn't get beyond his release address after he left Barlinnie.'

'Can I suggest that you try the DHSS?'

'Sorry?'

'The Department of Health and Social Security. They have a record of most of us in some form or another. You'll have to put it in writing and you may need a warrant before they'll release the information. They should be able to give you the address from which he last claimed Supplementary Benefit. You'll have to take it from there.'

'Yes, yes, I should have thought of that. I'll draft the letter before I go to Middleton's house.'

'You could also telephone them to warn them that the letter is on its way. Say it's a murder inquiry and that you're under time pressure. You never know your luck, they may ring back with the information, especially if you chance to speak to an unutterably bored clerical officer who'll jump at the chance to bring some excitement into her tedious day.'

'I'll give it a whirl.' Sussock rose from the chair.

'Oh, do more than that, Ray,' said Donoghue with an icy note in his voice. 'Pursue it relentlessly.'

'Yes, sir.'

'One further point of information, Ray. Friend Whannell is now believed to be sporting a beard, a red one. Probably a very striking figure.'

'What's the damage?' asked Montgomerie.

'You name it,' said the Ward Sister. She wore a crisp white uniform with an inverted watch hanging at the front. 'Both arms broken, both legs broken, wrists and ankles broken, ribs bruised, probably broken, a couple of teeth missing. No sign of internal injury, no sign of head injury.'

'Pretty methodical spanking,' Montgomerie said. 'Hardly the work of an amateur.'

'Offend somebody, did he?' said the Sister.

'Well, you could say that.'

'Pity. Nice-looking boy.'

'Try telling a swimmer that a shark is an elegant-looking fish.'

'I don't understand?'

'Well . . .' Then he thought the better of it. 'Can I go and talk to him?'

'Yes. But not too long. He'll tire easily in his condition.'

Montgomerie loped down the ward with long, effortless strides. He stopped by the bed in the corner where Wee Timmy the Rat lay with his arms and legs encased in heavy plaster and suspended above him. He smiled a sickly smile when he saw Montgomerie approach.

'Cops!' he snarled.

'You don't like the Police Force?'

'Not particularly.'

'Now why is that?' Montgomerie sat by the bed and plucked a grape from a bunch which lay on the bedside table.

'Help yourself,' said Wee Timmy the Rat. 'That's for me to know . . .'

'And for me to find out. I know,' Montgomerie replied. 'Strangely enough, young Timothy, that's why I'm here, to find things out. That's what I get paid to do. Fell down the stair, did you?'

'You're so funny you slay me, big man.'

'Glad you can laugh, young Timothy. Attitude is an important part of the cure.'

'That right?'

'Believe me.'

'Good. I'll sign myself out and just laugh myself back to health.'

'It's still a long process.'

'I thought there would be a catch.'

'So who did this?'

'Don't you know?'

'Yes. That's why I'm sitting here eating your grapes.'

'You're wise as well as funny. You should go in for the police force.'

'Oh, I aim to.'

'So go and get on with your work and let me laugh myself back to health.'

'Going to exact your own revenge, are you?'

'That's for me to know.'

'And for me to find out.' Montgomerie finished the sentence for him. 'This is getting to be a repetitious conversation.'

'So go and talk to someone else, dog breath.'

'You think I don't want to?'

Wee Timmy the Rat looked at the ceiling. His bed was in an old part of the Western Infirmary. The ward had a high vaulted ceiling and the sun shone in through the stained glass windows.

'Listen,' said Montgomerie. 'I'm not sure you understand your situation.'

'Oh, I understand it right enough.'

'Well, I'm going to put you in the picture anyway. We know about your moneylending activities, so don't start trying to hide anything. The men who attacked you also battered your old mother.'

Wee Timmy the Rat glanced at Montgomerie with alarm.

'Don't worry, she's OK. She's going home soon, just a case of concussion. She was kept in for observation. However, she's not going to like what she sees when she gets home.'

'What do you mean?'

'I saw it last night. I arrived just as they were lifting you on to a stretcher. They made a real mess of it, turned it over as though they were looking for something. Keep it under the bed, did you?'

'What?'

'The float. You know, the readies to finance your operation. If you did, it's not there now. I also heard some nasty things being said about you by the blokes in the street, such as the fact that you aren't going to be too safe in Maryhill no more. Your drogues have deserted you, Timmy, your money has all gone. You don't have any muscle any more.'

Wee Timmy the Rat went pale.

'So are you going to give me a lead or aren't you?'

Then Wee Timmy the Rat turned to Montgomerie and smiled in a way that Montgomerie had long learned to recognize meant bad news was coming his way.

'Try a cop.'

'What!'

'A cop called Bell.'

'What!' said Montgomerie again. 'What do you mean?'

So Wee Timmy the Rat told Montgomerie exactly what he meant.

Montgomerie pulled the door of Donoghue's office shut with a firm click and walked away down the corridor to the CID rooms. He knew that he had left Donoghue a worried man. Just then Sussock and Bell turned into the corridor, having climbed the stair from the ground floor and turned towards Donoghue's office. As they passed, Sussock and Montgomerie nodded to each other, Montgomerie said, 'Sarge,' but Bell saw in Montgomerie's eyes an undisguised glare of hostility directed at him. Bell faltered in his steps and then continued to follow Sussock.

Sussock tapped on Donoghue's office door. There was the customary pause, though Sussock thought it was longer than usual, before Donoghue said, 'Come in.' Sussock pushed the door open and he and Bell entered Donoghue's office.

'He's not there,' began Sussock as he walked from the door to Donoghue's desk. Bell followed sheepishly. His legs felt weak and his heart was pounding. Bell glanced up and saw that he was the subject of a cold and angry stare from Donoghue.

'Not there?' Donoghue turned to Sussock.

'No, sir. There's no answer to the door. We went round the house and looked in the windows. You can see inside all the rooms, it being a bungalow, and all the curtains being open. Well, like I said, he's not at home. I checked with the Post Office, he's not there. As far as they are concerned, he's following a direction to remain at home and to be ready to make himself available for the Post office's internal inquiry.'

'Any sign of him having left the house for good? I mean wardrobe doors left open, drawers hanging open?'

Sussock shook his head. 'No, sir. His car is still in the garage. His neighbour was out gardening, she saw him yesterday but had not seen him this morning. She said he didn't look as though he was going anywhere. He may have gone out, of course, to the shops, to visit a relative, he's not under house arrest, but I have an odd feeling about this. I don't normally get such feelings, but in this case . . .'

'I don't think they're misplaced, Ray.' Donoghue leaned back in his chair. 'Take a seat, please, I'd like a word with you.' Sussock sat, a worried look coming over his face. 'Bell,' continued Donoghue, 'I wonder if you would excuse us.'

'Certainly, sir.' Bell turned towards the door.

'Oh, and Bell . . .'

'Sir?'

'Remain close by, please. I'll be wanting a word with you as well.'

'Certainly, sir.' Bell left Donoghue's office, pulling the door shut behind him, and the two officers heard him walk quickly away down the corridor.

'It's trouble, Ray,' said Donoghue, leaning forward again and taking his pipe from the ashtray.

'Oh.' Sussock remained impassive, but he was frantically searching his mind for the 'trouble'. His health perhaps? Time for another medical? Surely not already. His extended service being revoked; gold watch and chain coming his way?

'Yes,' said Donoghue. 'Makes me feel sick. Just when I was looking forward to a half day with my wife and children. I'm still taking the leave, but I shan't enjoy it.'

'Just tell me straight.' Sussock braced himself.

'I can't,' said Donoghue. 'There's nothing to tell

straight, it's just that the one allegation I most fear has been levelled at one of our team.'

'Who's saying what?'

'About whom is the pertinent point,' said Donoghue, scraping blackened ash from his pipe. 'Young DC Bell is the subject.'

'Ding-Dong?' said Sussock.

'It's an appropriate nickname,' said Donoghue. 'Alarm bells are ringing all over the shop.'

'In respect of what? Poor motivation. I know I brought that to your attention this morning, but I didn't expect you to be so worried about it.'

'If that were his only problem.'

'What do you mean?'

'Earlier this morning, Montgomerie interviewed a moneylender who was worked over last night. Claims the thugs who did it were sent by our Mr Bell. Claims it was in retaliation for an incident a few days ago when the moneylender's apes had Bell worked over for failing to pay off a debt. The moneylender had his claws into Bell for four thousand pounds.'

'Oh my God.' Sussock slumped back into the chair.

'The moneylender—Montgomerie was investigating him for a possible extortion charge—the moneylender said that Bell had, maybe still has, a big gambling problem, gets into debt, borrows to get out of debt, and the downward spiral begins.'

'Is that why his marriage broke up?'

'Who's to say, but it certainly wouldn't have helped it.'

'Well, that's Bell finished if the moneylender can prove anything.'

'That's not the issue, Ray.'

'It isn't?'

'No. According to the moneylender, Middleton, the man from whose house you have just returned, also has a big gambling problem. The moneylender has his claws into Middleton for a good few quid. Middleton and Bell are both members of Gamblers Anonymous.'

Sussock groaned. 'They are both previously known to each other. Why didn't he say something? He would have been taken off the case if he'd declared that he knew Middleton socially. He need not have said anything about his gambling problems. That would have remained his secret.'

'It's not that simple, Ray.'

'Oh?'

'No.' Donoghue put his pipe down. 'You know, I don't feel like a smoke. No, according to the moneylender, Middleton and friend Bell set up the Post Office job between them.'

Sussock sat in a stunned silence and Donoghue couldn't help wringing his hands.

Eventually Donoghue broke the silence. 'The theory's sound. They both know each other, they both have money problems, they both have access to inside information, Middleton on timing and procedure of cash deliveries, Bell on criminal experience and availability. He had access to police files and could have put a formidable team together. Once the job has been pulled the gang sit it out in a safe house, Middleton sweats it out at home full of hurt innocence and eventually gets another post, and Bell keeps tabs on the investigation, either to give the neds the tip-off if we get too close, or to frustrate our efforts from the inside. Probably both.'

'Neat and simple and utterly sickening,' said Sussock.

'Isn't it.'

'The only favour they seem to have done us was to recruit this clown Whannell. He's already exposed the murder of Middleton's wife by his indiscretion; by his greed, hoping to make a few quid by selling the antique shot-guns, he's also indicated that the safe house in question may well be in Ayrshire. He's the weak link in their chain. We have to go for him, put everything into tracing him.'

'Right, sir.'

'It's an unsettling feeling,' said Donoghue, at last succumbing and taking up his pipe.

'What is, sir?'

'Not knowing how much of what we know, they also know.' He flicked his gold plated lighter and played the flame over the bowl. 'All these years I've been used to being privy to my own information.'

'Yes. It makes you suspicious of every act of Bell's,' mused Sussock. 'Like the 'phone call he made from Campbeltown yesterday. He could well have been warning the gang that we were about to lift Middleton. He must have known that Middleton wouldn't stand up to interrogation.'

'So Middleton's in the safe house?'

'Probably, sir.'

'Probably, Ray?'

'Probably. I wouldn't like to speculate. There's enough speculation flying around as it is.'

'I agree. So what shall I do about Bell?'

'The most difficult question of all, that one, sir,' stuttered Sussock, nonplussed and mollified at the same time about being asked his opinion. 'Dare say we have to inform the old man.'

'Dare say you're right,' said Donoghue. 'What do you think we should do with Bell?'

'Basically there's two choices. We can say nothing and keep an eye on him, or we can bring him in now and confront him with the allegation. That would give him the right to reply before you went to see the Chief Superintendent. He might even want to go with you.'

'You'd like that, would you, Ray?' I mean if the allegation was directed at you?'

'Yes, sir, I think I would.'

'Very well, we'll do that, if only to hedge our bets. If we keep an eye on him it gives him time to continue to pass information if that's what he's doing.' Donoghue picked up the 'phone on his desk and dialled a two-figure internal number. 'Ah, Montgomerie,' he said as his call was answered. 'Bell there? . . . no? . . . I see. Thank you.' He replaced the receiver and dialled another internal number. 'Front desk? DI Donoghue. Did DC Bell say where he was going? He didn't? Thank you.' He replaced the receiver and looked at Sussock. 'You may have gathered that the bird has flown. Seemed to be in a tearing hurry, according to Hamilton on the front desk.'

'Well, that about clinches it,' said Sussock, a weary note to his voice.

'Let's just say it doesn't augur well.' Donoghue drummed his fingers on his desk. 'Ray, I'm leaving you holding the fort this afternoon, I'm taking my leave. It's only a half day, dammit. I'm going to see Findlater and then I'm going to make a call in connection with the case. I'll be in tomorrow at eight-thirty sharp.'

'Very good, sir.'

'It does you good to re-charge your batteries,' Donoghue said, convincing himself. 'Remember to keep chewing away at the Whannell connection, he's the key. Put King and Abernethy in the picture and you can take Montgomerie off the moneylender case. I guess that's all wrapped up now anyway.'

'Yes, sir. I was going to send someone round to see Mr Anderson.'

'Who . . .'

'Flora Middleton's brother, sir. I mean, now that we have the positive identification.'

'Oh yes, yes. I should have thought of that. Nevertheless Whannell gets priority.'

Donoghue had a half-hour audience with Findlater and

left the P Division building at 12.30 p.m. He drove from the Police Station to an address in North Kelvinside. .

'Mr McGeechie?' said Donoghue, as the old man shuffled to one side, opening the door of his flat. 'DI Donoghue. My young colleague, Mr Abernethy, called on you last Thursday in connection with the robbery at Maryhill Post Office.'

'I remember,' said McGeechie. 'Come in, young man, come in.'

When they were standing in McGeechie's flat Donoghue said, 'I want to ask you about a specific point, if I may, Mr McGeechie. You said that you saw the estate car arrive and then the occupants transported themselves and their goods into a delivery van which then drove off.'

'That is correct.'

'Later, you say, a police officer arrived and approached the abandoned estate car?'

'Aye, that he did. He was in ordinary clothes.'

'Now, do take your time before answering. Did the police officer who approached the car enter the vehicle?'

'No.'

'You sure?'

'Aye, sir.'

'His prints were inside the car,' mused Donoghue.

'Sorry?' said the old man. 'I didn't catch . . . .'

'Oh, nothing,' replied Donoghue, 'just talking to myself.' He looked out of Mr McGeechie's window. 'Fine view you have.'

'Aye, I like watching the birds in the trees.'

'Blackbird on that tree, there,' said Donoghue.

The old man peered out of the window. 'Where? I can't see him.'

Donoghue sighed.

'It's a wee thrush,' said Mr McGeechie.

Inside his Rover, Donoghue gripped the steering-wheel. He felt a mixture of grave disappointment and satisfaction. 'That clinches it,' he said to himself.

'You the polis, aye?'

Montgomerie turned from his lager and looked down at the man who suddenly stood beside him. The man was short, slightly built, with greasy dirty hair and a tacky overcoat. He needed a bath, he could use a shave. He wanted a drink.

'Maybe.' Montgomerie turned back to his lager. He didn't want to be a cop. The allegation about Bell had upset him, standing at the window of the CID rooms and watching Bell flee the Police Station and hail a passing cab had sickened him. His duty turn had finished at 2.30 p.m. He wrote up and signed out and hit the Gay Gordon at 3.00 p.m. By 3.15 he was already on his third pint. He didn't want to be a cop. He didn't need the pushy little dosser at his left elbow. So he said, 'Push off!'

'No, I got information, chief.'

'You've got information, have you?'

'That's me, chief.'

'Suppose I don't wnat any information.'

'You'd be an unusual polis if you didn't, sir.'

'I haven't said I'm a policeman.'

'You are, though.'

'That certain, are you?'

'Aye.'

'Look, take a hike, Jim.'

'You don't know what you're turning down.'

'Whatever it is I don't want it. Look, you know where the Police Station is? Go there.'

'So you are a polis, aye. I'm always right.'

'Aye.' Montgomerie drained his glass. 'Same again boss.'

The man at his elbow drew a sharp breath between his teeth.

There were a few punters in the bar, sitting on the low

plastic bench which ran round the wall, their drinks standing before them on the narrow tables. They made their drinks last and kept a respectable distance from each other. They didn't speak. Above the gantry there was a television with both the sound and the colour turned up too loud. It was showing a horse race in England. Another world.

'Good stuff,' said the man.

'You still here?' said Montgomerie. He saw the man's eyes widen and his jaw drop a fraction. Montgomerie turned and paid the barman for his drink. He turned again and was about to say, 'All right, what have you got?' but found he was alone. Montgomerie looked around. There was no sign of the man, who appeared to have left the bar as silently as he had appeared. Montgomerie thought he maybe ought not to have spoken as he had. The guy had been out of luck, bumping into him in the mood he was in.

His children were running on ahead. Hundreds of feet below them were the cold grey waters of the Firth of Forth. Above them were the reaching vertical columns and arcing hawsers of the suspension bridge. The Donoghues had driven from their Edinburgh home, had left their car at South Queensferry and were walking across the road bridge to North Queensferry where the children would search under the russet tubes of the railway bridge for coins which had been thrown out of the railway carriage windows, for luck, by people observing the old and endearing custom. While their children scrambled over the rocks, Mr and Mrs Donoghue would take tea and hot buns in a café. But at that moment they walked along the road bridge. He looked east. She looked west.

'Christ!' She suddenly turned to him. 'It's once in a blue moon that you get time off duty during the school holidays, now that you've got half a day you might at least make some effort to be friendly. We'd like a father and a husband to drive the car, not a chauffeur.'

'Something's bothering me,' he said. 'Something at work. I get silent when I'm bothered about something.'

'You're telling me!' said the woman.

Montgomerie staggered out of the Gay Gordon. The visual impact of old Glasgow town wasn't lessened any by the alcohol numbing his brain; the old dark tenements, the rubble and fires on the gap sites, the new housing in the distance, the head of a dead dog sticking out of a refuse bag. There was a low grey sky and the drizzle was falling again.

'Hi, polis.' The small man with the grubby raincoat leaned against a lamp-post.

'You still here?'

'You forgotten, aye?'

'What?' Montgomerie pulled his coat collar up against the damp. He took a packet of cigarettes from his pocket and offered one to the little guy.

'What it was you were drinking to forget,' said the little guy, plucking a fag from Montgomerie's packet. Montgomerie started to grin. 'You're a right bloody liability for a guy to have around, aren't you? Have you forgotten it then, by Christ?' The wee man grinned, warmly.

'What do they call you, Jim?' Montgomerie took a cigarette for himself and lit it. 'And what have you got for us?'

'Tuesday Noon is the name and what I've got is a feller trying to unload some guns. Fancy guns, shot-guns, in a smart case, all up and down Maryhill and away into the Barracks, down by Bridgeton and around the Barrows last Saturday. He's some brass neck, like the Firearms Act doesn't exist.'

'That right?'

'Aye. Worth something, is it?'

'Could be. Let's go to that 'phone box. I'd like you to meet a friend of mine.'

'Maybe we could wait in the bar?' said Tuesday Noon.

CHAPTER 9

Wednesday, October 16, 3.15 p.m.

The mortuary attendant parted the shroud and revealed the man's face. It was thinner than in life, it had an odd grey hue and Sussock could see a bruise on the forehead.

'It's Middleton all right,' said Sussock and stepped backwards.

The mortuary assistant covered the face again and slid the drawer shut.

'Cause of death?' Sussock turned to the tall, silver-haired pathologist who had accompanied him to the mortuary.

'Shall we step into the office here?' suggested Reynolds.

In the office Dr Reynolds sat behind his desk. It was an old desk, the office was cluttered and small. There was little light. Sussock remained standing because Reynolds sat on the only chair. The pathologist took a file from his briefcase and laid it on the desk. 'Just notes at the moment,' he said. 'I'll be sending the completed report up to you by the pony express once it has been typed.'

'Very good, sir,' said Sussock.

'I believe the deceased's effects have been forwarded to you by the police at Greenock.'

'They arrived just after lunch, sir. A courier brought them.'

'Yes, well, I performed the post mortem about an hour ago. Cause of death was massive internal injury consistent with a fall from a great height.'

'Not drowning?'

'No.' Reynolds shook his head. 'I know he was found on the banks of the river at low tide, but no, I had a peek inside his lungs, there was some water there, but nothing like the amount you'd get in a drowning victim. My guess is that he was killed on entry, at which point his lungs just stopped working.' Reynolds paused, studied his notes and then began to report in a detached, dispassionate way. 'Yes, there were fractures, we did a skeletal survey, most of his bones were broken. You'd get that with a fall on to water. Above a certain height there's actually very little difference in the damage caused by falling on to water and falling on to concrete. He seems to have fallen head first, the top of his skull was virtually caved in, extensive brain damage, I'd say that killed him, that alone I mean, over and above the other damage. Lesion on the left side caused by the tearing effect of water. It's only the second time that I've seen such an injury. Oh yes, he was still wearing handcuffs, with his wrists behind his back, one was tight around the wrist, the other side of the handcuff was loose, as though it hadn't been snapped on properly.'

'Or not taken off properly?'

'Yes. Mind you, that's a job for you. As far as pathology is concerned, the implication is that in the unlikely event of his surviving the fall, he would have drowned anyway.'

'How long was he in the water, sir?'

'Not long. Skin tissue is still intact, no sign of bloating through the build-up of internal gases, extremities not nibbled at by sea creatures. Couple of hours, possibly. Dumped when the tide was turning and was deposited on the mudbanks soon afterwards. Lay there till he was found in the early morning by a fellow out digging up lugworms, or so I believe.'

'You say he would have had to fall from a great height to sustain injuries such as these?'

'The use of a helicopter being too fanciful for serious consideration, I believe that this man's injuries were caused by his being dropped into the Clyde from a bridge. There are a number of bridges across the river, but the only one high enough to allow a fall which would produce this sort of damage is the Erskine Bridge, two hundred and eighty feet high and about a mile upstream from where the body was found.'

'Has to be, I reckon,' said Sussock.

'I only say this because I happen to be au fait with the area.'

'I appreciate that, sir.'

'Whether he was murdered or whether he committed an elaborate form of suicide to suggest that he was murdered is really a job for you chaps, but it was either murder or suicide. The barrier along the walkway of the bridge is too high and wide for him to have fallen over by accident; he would have had to make a conscious and determined attempt to clamber over the barrier, which would be well nigh impossible with his wrists shackled behind his back, or . . .'

'Or else he was manhandled over the top,' said Sussock.

Reynolds nodded. 'Exactly.'

'Is a mushroom a place for training husky dogs?' Tuesday Noon jabbed Montgomerie's ribs and sniggered.

Montgomerie smiled politely.

Tuesday Noon picked up his glass, drained it, and then looked at Montgomerie with wide eyes.

'No,' said Montgomerie. 'That's three you've had, Tuesday. My mate will buy you some more.' Montgomerie's speech was getting slurred.

Tuesday Noon and he had gone back to the Gay Gordon after Montgomerie had made the 'phone call. King took the call and said that he and Abernethy would be right up. That was an hour ago. In that time Tuesday

Noon had proved to be a bar-room comic who could put them away, at great expense to Montgomerie, who felt he should have taken the wee guy straight back to P Division despite the smell on his breath. As it was, he had now sunk six lagers without the benefit of lunch, and the only thing he could do was to sit and wait for King and Abernethy. Going into the Police Station after two glasses of lager was one thing, going in when you were as tight as a tick was quite another. 'Just make it last, Tuesday,' he said.

'Make what last, Mr Montgomerie? It's all gone.'

'No more, Tuesday. Got to keep your head clear.'

In the CID rooms at P Division it had been like this:

'Selling shot-guns in the bars in Maryhill, you say.' King stood at his desk still wearing his overcoat, having just come in for duty. He beckoned to Abernethy.

'That's right,' said Montgomerie. 'And around other places, hawking them all over Big G he is, by all accounts. He's standing with me now.'

'Know him?'

'No, never met him before. Tuesday Noon by name.'

'What?'

'Tuesday Noon.'

'How did he get a name like that?'

'I don't know, Richard, and right now I don't particularly care. It's a question you can put to him.'

'All right. How does he look, any previous?'

'Wouldn't surprise me.'

'I'll check the records. You bringing him in, aye?'

'I'd rather not.'

'What sort of attitude is that? I know you're off duty but . . . well, for heaven's sake, Ray Sussock's at the mortuary, you'll never guess who is thought to have taken a power dive into the Clyde . . .'

'Middleton, perchance.'

'Perchance you are correct. How did you know?'

'I took the call from Greenock Police and passed the message on to Ray Sussock; all they had then was the name in the wallet.'

'Yeah, I was forgetting. Anyway Ray's out, Fabian's taken a half day, and there's only me and Abernethy left to cover, so why can't you bring him in? Anyway, where's Ding-Dong?'

'The answer to your last question is a tale in itself,' said Montgomerie. 'The answer to your first question is that said Tuesday Noon does not wish to enter a police . . .'

'That's his problem,' said King. 'Get a grip, Mal, bounce the bugger in.'

'I'd be inclined to meet him half way on this, I get the impression . . .'

'Malcolm, you're hedging.'

'Well, since you mention it, Dick, while I'm not exactly legless, I have been gently quaffing since I finished work and what with missing lunch I'd rather . . .'

'I see, all right, we'll be right up.'

'Good man. I'm in a bar called the Gay Gordon on Garscube Road near the Round Toll.'

'We'll be right up,' said King again and put the 'phone down. As he did it instantly rang again.

'DHSS for Sergeant Sussock,' said PC Piper, who was manning the switchboard.

'He's not in,' said King. 'What's it about?'

The line clicked, there was a moment's silence and then Piper said, 'Whannell, sir.'

'Put them on, please,' said King.

There was another click, Piper's voice was heard to say, 'Go ahead now, please,' and then a thin female voice said 'Hello.'

'DC King here. It's about Whannell, I understand?'

'Oh yes,' said the thin female voice. 'Only I was told to ask for Mr Sussock.'

'He's engaged at the moment,' replied King, relaxing

his own voice when he sensed he was talking to a nervous person. 'I'm aware of his request, you talk to me.'

'I can?'

'Yes,' said King. 'If you would, it is a matter of urgency.'

'Oh, only I don't want to be caught out. I shouldn't be doing this.'

'What?'

' 'Phone out with this sort of information. It's secret, no, what's the word, confidential, even from the police.'

'The source of the information will remain a closely guarded secret. What can you tell us?'

'About Whannell, do you mean?'

'Yes,' said King patiently.

'Well, I did it over lunch-break. I looked up the files. I found a Whannell who fits the details that Mr Sussock gave me, his age and that. He's forty-five now.'

'Whannell, you mean?'

'Who else?'

'Nothing. Carry on, please.'

'Well yes, he lived at that address in Clouston Street. I've been there, ugh, how people can . . . anyway he was there, now he's not, and so . . .'

'What's his current address?'

'We have his last address on file . . . oh well, if that's what you want you get it, mind you I reckon scarlet's the best, like when Susie had her birthday . . .'

'What the hell?' said King.

'She looked smashing in that red dress . . . I'm sorry, you still there?'

'Yes,' said King, less patiently.

'Only the EO walked past.'

'The EO?'

'Executive Officer, on his stick. Sort of hobbled by my desk. That's why I went on about scarlet dresses and that. Honestly, he's a grumpy old cretin. I made all that up.'

'About Whannell?'

'No, about Susie. I don't know any Susie, it came right into my head . . .'

'The address!'

'Oh aye, well, Whannell, care of Duncan, seven-fifty-three Tresta Road, in Cadder that is.'

'Thank you.'

'Oh, you're welcome,' said the woman like she'd heard in the films, but by then King had already put the 'phone down.

'Get you're coat on, Abernethy,' he said.

'It's on already.'

'So it is.'

King and Abernethy left P Division Police Station in an unmarked car. They drove along Sauchiehall Street, solid Victorian houses converted into offices, a couple of hotels, and chic basement restaurants. They joined Dumbarton Road and drove past the Kelvin Hall, turned right up Church Street and into Byres Road: University land, Bohemian and Bourgeoisie, bearded men and denim-clad mothers carrying babies in papooses, supermarkets, pubs, little shops selling incense, Rubik cubes and 'executive toys'. Above the shops on either side of the road were three storeys of solid stone tenements. The car bounced across Great Western Road, the four-lane westering artery, and King drove up Queen Margaret Drive and emerged into a vast gentle hillside of rubble and weeds which led up to Maryhill Road, snaking along the watershed. This was G20, where the old tenements were being refurbished and those beyond redemption demolished, leaving yawning gap sites where the neds dumped and incinerated the liberated motors. King turned left on Maryhill Road, into the tenements, the new shopping centre, the old railway tunnel, and then turned right by the Job Centre and drove past the scrapyard and under the single lane canal bridge which pre-dates all that which has been built and later demolished around it. King and Abernethy emerged into the Cadder, a grey pebbledashed scheme planted on the hillside between the canal and the Western Necropolis. Tresta Road was the top drag in the Cadder. Seven-fifty-three was down the bottom end.

It looked bust up and beaten up. The garden was overgrown, the curtains were shut, a couple of windows had been put through and sheets of cardboard had been thrust in their place. King and Abernethy pushed open the metal gate and walked up the path. The name on the door was 'Duncan'. King pressed the bell. It didn't seem to work, so he rapped on the door. There was no sound from inside the house. He rapped again and this time he heard someone stirring, footsteps on the stair. Then the door was opened by a woman. She had a drawn face, deeply indented with lines on her brow. Her cheeks were hollow. Her hair was white and hung on her head like a mop. King guessed she was about thirty-five.

'Mrs Duncan?' he said.

'Miss Duncan,' she replied after a while.

'Detective-Constables King and Abernethy, P Division.' He showed the woman his I/D but she seemed to be permanently staring into the middle distance. 'We're trying to trace a man called Whannell.'

'He's no' here.'

'Expecting him back?'

'Don't know what to expect any more, sir.'

'Don't call me sir,' said King. 'Mr King will do nicely.'

'Yes,' said Miss Duncan.

'Does he live here or not?'

The woman shook her head.

'What is he, relative, a friend?'

The woman looked at King and then, after an overlong pause, said, 'He rented a room.'

'Rented a room?'

There was another long pause while the woman seemed to be formulating her answer. Then she said, 'Yes.' There was a glassy look in her eyes. King reckoned she was heavily tranquillized. 'It's all right,' added the woman, 'I have permission from the factor to rent my rooms.'

'We wouldn't klype anyway,' said King.

The woman smiled at King. She seemed to King to put a lot of effort into making the smile.

'Has he quit?'

The woman shook her head.

'He's still got a room here, then.' There was a note of excitement in King's voice.

'Aye,' said Miss Duncan. 'But he owes rent.'

'Can we take a look?'

'Aye,' said the woman and with slow, deliberate movements turned and walked down the hall. The two cops followed her in. The house was stuffy with stale air, the carpet in the hall was worn and soiled into a sticky layer of something covering the floor. The woman walked through the house and then sat in the kitchen resting her arm on the table. There was half a bottle of milk, the remains of a sliced loaf, the outer slices, curled and hard. Greasy plates lay in the sink. The woman looked up and seemed surprised to see the two cops standing in front of her. 'Oh,' she said. 'You're here.'

'Which is his room, hen?' asked Abernethy.

'Top of the stairs,' she said. 'The first door.'

King and Abernethy went up the stairs. They opened the first door cautiously. It was dark. King switched on the light. A mean bulb without a shade glowed dimly and revealed a single unmade bed pushed into the corner, a chest of drawers, old newspapers for floor covering. The two cops began to search the room, searching the drawers, rummaging in the waste-bin.

'Seems to have done a moonlight,' said Abernethy,

sifting the articles along the window-ledge. An old glass tumbler, dusty and grimy, a comb, a railway ticket from Glasgow to Dunlop. He picked it up, 'This any good, Dick?'

King turned and looked at the ticket. He turned it over in his hand. 'Gold dust, my son,' he said. 'Pure gold dust.'

They went back downstairs. In the kitchen Miss Duncan still sat in the same chair with the same arm resting on the table. She turned slowly and looked at the two cops.

'I might go to my bed,' she said. 'Give me something to do.'

'When did you last see Mr Whannell?' asked King.

'I don't know, sir.' She laboured each word. 'Long, long time, maybe two weeks, long time. When is he coming back? He owes rent.'

'I don't think he is,' said King.

So Miss Duncan started to cry.

In the car Abernethy turned to King. 'What now?' he asked.

King drummed his fingers on the steering-wheel. He thought and then replied, 'I think we go and log this ticket. Whannell was seen driving a pick-up belonging to a farm in Ayrshire, chances are it's near Dunlop.'

'You're not forgetting about Malcolm?'

'I had until just now. He'll just have to sit tight until we can get there. He's in a bar, it's hardly an onerous duty.'

'Yes, but he's done his whack for today.'

'That's right,' said King, starting the car, 'he's now sitting in a bar.'

'I had to come.' Bell sat in the chair next to the fire. He blew on his hands and rubbed them together. The old house was cold because Izzy wouldn't allow a fire, except at night. It was colder inside the house than it was outside and it was cold enough outside as the October winds scythed across the exposed Ayrshire hillside.

'So what happened?' growled Izzy.

'They were on to me. I got out just in time.'

'Followed?'

Bell shook his head. 'Hailed a cab in Charing Cross, took it to Central Station. Got the first train out. Stayed low in the bar until it was time to catch the train. I wasn't followed.'

'Didn't call at your flat, then?'

'No. I just fled.'

'How do you know they were on to you?'

'I saw the way one of them looked at me.'

'Is that all!'

'I could tell, Izzy.' Bell shivered. 'Believe me, I know. I know a cop's suspicious look, you can read their faces. He was a young cop, he couldn't disguise his look. If he could I'd have been banged up by now. Always been friendly to me, this guy, but this morning he looked at me like I was a criminal.'

'You are,' said the big man.

'Aye.' Bell nodded. 'I suppose I am.' Bell hadn't noticed before just how big Izzy was. Maybe it was his short legs that made Izzy look small, but when he sat in a chair, all Bell could see was a vast chest, wide shoulders, and icy eyes above a bushy beard. Bell got scared. 'Wouldn't be putting another job together, would you?'

'I might,' said Izzy. 'Not for a while.'

'I could be of use.' Bell grinned hopefully.

'Can't see how,' said Izzy, ending the subject.

Seaweed shuffled and then sat down in a chair against the far wall. Bell nodded at him and smiled. Seaweed remained stone-faced. There were two women in the room, Izzy's women; they didn't talk, they just looked at Bell with undisguised pity. Even Bunny, sitting by the window watching the road, avoided looking at Bell.

'Sorry, Matthew,' said Izzy, 'but we'll need to move on.

Whannell's away, do you see?'

'Hey, Izzy,' said Bell.

King and Abernethy found Sussock writing up in his office. It was 4.30 p.m. He held up the railway ticket. 'One return to Dunlop.'

'So?'

'Found in the room rented by Whannell. I took a message from the DHSS for you.'

'I see. I take it he no longer stays there?'

'Well, he hasn't quit, but he's got little or nothing to come back to.'

'Done a moonlight all right,' said Abernethy.

'But this ties in with the address on the side of the pick-up Whannell is thought to have been driving,' said Sussock.

'That's what we thought, Sarge,' said King. 'Narrows it down a bit. A farm near Dunlop.'

'Narrows it down a bit right enough.' Sussock nodded. 'I suggest you 'phoned down to the police in Kilmarnock, I think that's the nearest big town, and explain things. See if they've noticed any activity of an unusual nature around any farm in the area. We'll bring it up at the review meeting tomorrow.'

'I didn't know there was one,' said King.

'Fabian just 'phone in from his home. Asked me to arrange it for nine o'clock sharp.'

'Is there no let-up?' said Abernethy.

'Let-up? What's that?' replied King.

Sussock grinned. 'Well, that's me for the day,' he said. 'I was just waiting on you two coming back.' He stood and reached for his coat and battered old trilby.

'Fine, sarge,' said King. He turned to Abernethy. 'Do you want to 'phone down to Kilmarnock? I'll go and find Malcolm.'

*

King drove the unmarked car back up to the Round Toll and parked it in the dim side street next to the Gay Gordon.

'So you deigned to come at last,' said Montgomerie as King approached him.

'Held up,' replied King, sitting on a stool opposite Montgomerie.

'This is Tuesday Noon.' Montgomerie indicated the man sitting next to him. Tuesday Noon eyed King warmly. 'This is Mr King.'

King and Tuesday Noon nodded at each other.

'And I will now leave you at it,' said Montgomerie angrily. 'I do have a private life to attend to.' He made a show of storming out of the bar but really just staggered towards the door.

'So what have you got, Tuesday?' said King.

'Not a thing,' said Tuesday Noon and pushed his empty glass towards King.

'Whisky, aye,' said King.

'Double, aye,' said Tuesday Noon.

King bought him a single hit. Tuesday Noon didn't hide his disappointment.

'So now what do you have?' said King.

'Just like I told Mr Montgomerie there. Man selling guns, trying to unload them in bars.'

'Description?'

'A bit short, a bit fat, forty, maybe fifty, has a beard.'

'Name?'

'Joe.' Tuesday Noon threw back the whisky and pushed the empty glasses towards King. King ignored it. There was a silence.

Eventually King said, 'That's it, is it?'

'That's it.' Tuesday Noon grinned. 'I reckon that's worth something.'

'I reckon it's worth nothing,' said King. He took a plain white card from his jacket and wrote a telephone number on it. He pushed it across the table towards Tuesday Noon. 'If you get any more on this guy—' King rose from the table—' 'phone me. We want to know where he stays, better still 'phone us when he's on the street, tell us where he is. If you do that then maybe there's a drink in it for you.'

Thursday, October 17, 10.30 a.m.

Half an hour after the review meeting, Montgomerie and Sussock left their car and climbed the tiled close to Matthew 'Ding-Dong' Bell's flat. They stood on the stone landing three floors up. It was a quiet close, scrubbed and disinfected stairs, metal banisters with a polished wooden rail, solid storm doors in the front of each flat. Montgomerie pressed the door buzzer. 'Just in case,' he said.

Sussock grunted his approval. Up the stair a door opened and shut, a young woman came down carrying a small child on one arm and a shopping-bag on the other. She smiled at the two cops as she turned on the landing, going down the stair.

'I think we'll presume he's out, shall we, Sarge?' said Montgomerie as he fished into his pocket for a bunch of keys.

'It would surprise me if he was at home,' Sussock replied drily.

'Me too, Sarge,' said Montgomerie as he turned a key gently in one of the locks on the flat door. 'One down and two to go.' He studied the second lock. 'You know, it sticks in my craw to do this.'

'Aye, but he knew the risks.'

'That's it!' Montgomerie pushed the door open.

It was dark and stuffy inside Bell's flat. The curtains were shut and the windows were closed. Montgomerie negotiated the living-room floor and opened one of the curtains. Light flooded into the flat revealing the smashed hi-fi, the splintered screen of the television, torn cushions on the suite, books spilled from the shelves, upturned plants, soil and compost lying on the carpet.

'Someone's been here before us,' said Sussock. Montgomerie shook his head. 'I don't think so, Sarge. I've a feeling that this is the work of Wee Timmy the Rat, before he fell from grace.'

'Grace!'

'Power then, you know what I mean. What do you think about the furnishings, the standard of decoration, I mean if you can imagine it before the visitation of the little moneylender?'

'Nothing exceptional,' said Sussock. 'He seems to have got everything, but it's all modest. A regular cop's flat, I'd say.'

'Me too,' said Montgomerie. 'No indication of private means.'

'Oh, I see what you're driving at,' replied Sussock. 'No, there isn't, but we've only been here fifteen seconds.'

'What's he got here?'

'Rooms?'

'Aye.'

'Looks like just the bedroom after this. There'll also be a kitchen and bathroom.'

'I'll go and root around the bedroom. Do you want to make a start in here?'

'We'd better stick together, Sarge,' said Montgomerie. 'You know, corroboration.'

The bedroom was sparsely decorated. There was a single bed pushed against the wall, with a minium amount of blankets, a threadbare rug on the floor. In the wardrobe were a few casual clothes, half a dozen shirts, two pairs of trousers, a pullover. Under the bed was a pair of shoes, battered and already re-soled and getting thin again. There was an old chair in the corner. The light-bulb hung from the ceiling and was surrounded by an old yellow flower-patterned glass shade in which lay the bodies of half a dozen files. The walls were bare, fading cream paint on the cracked plaster.

'I reckon he must have been renting,' said Montgomerie. 'A short term measure, he'd be bringing the rest of his gear over from Edinburgh in due course. You know, once he was sorted out.'

'Aye,' Sussock nodded. 'I reckon that's it.'

But both men knew that DC Bell had just been revealed to be a very lonely man. Montgomerie and Sussock left the bedroom and Sussock, last to leave, pulled the door shut with a reverently gentle click, a gesture of apology for exposing that which Matthew Bell had sought to conceal.

In the main room they found an address book. It was a thick book, but had few entries, most were simply Christian names. In the front cover of the book were some letters which seemed faded and old. Sussock slipped them back inside the book. He continued to turn the pages and eventually came across an entry which read: Big Stevie, Gamblers Anon. It was accompanied by a telephone number.

Sussock knelt, picked up the telephone which lay on the floor and dialled the number. Montgomerie turned from the drawers in the wall unit and watched. When he had finished dialling, Sussock waited for a few moments and then said, 'Can I talk to Big Stevie, please . . . I am? Good, this is Detective-Sergeant Sussock, CID, P Division, I wonder if I could have a word with you about someone I think you may know through Gamblers Anonymous . . . Yes, yes, I appreciate that, sir, confidentiality will be respected and I can assure you that you would be helping this gentleman if you did cooperate . . . Yes, it's Matthew Bell . . . Well, that's right, he is a colleague of mine and we are anxious to resolve what appears to be a matter of some delicacy . . .'

'Delicacy!' said Montgomerie. Sussock glared at him.

'Yes, sir,' said Sussock. 'I know where it is . . . About eleven, before it gets too crowded, yes, sir. Thank you.' Sussock put the 'phone down. 'Don't be so bloody sarcastic, you.'

'Sarcastic, Sarge?'

'You know what I mean. What time is it?'

Montgomerie glanced at his watch. 'Coming up to eleven o'clock, Sarge.'

'Later than I thought. Fancy a drink, Montgomerie?'

'Why not?'

'Good. You're buying. The Auld Hoose on Maryhill Road. If you've never been there you're in for a treat.'

The Auld Hoose was in fact quite a new hoose. It was a modern Glasgow bar which seemed to draw its architectural heritage from the pillboxes of the Second World War. It was made of concrete, it was squat, square and solid. The doors were metal and inside there was no natural light. The tartan-patterned carpet was permanently soggy from spilled drink. The colour television flashed the test card from a position high in one corner of the room. The gantry ran the length of one wall and the punters sat in little cubicles round the other three walls. The rest of the floor area was standing room only. It was a false world of cold comfort, a place where you could shut yourself off from the realities of life on the dole, a place where you can be lulled into parting with your money. Walking through the metal doors of the Auld Hoose was the quickest escape from Glasgow.

The doors were opened at 11.00 a.m. and they would stay open until leaving time at 11.00 p.m. Sussock and Mongomerie entered the bar at five minutes after eleven. There were already one or two punters in there, a young boy studying form, a couple of oldies in flat caps sitting together with their hands on their knees looking at the wee heavy on the table in front of each of them, as though it was an object of veneration. In the corner amid the wisps of smoke which still hung in the bar since the doors last shut twelve hours ago was a well-set man. He looked at the two cops. They approached him. 'Big Stevie?' said Sussock.

'Aye,' said Big Stevie.

'DC Montgomerie, I'm Detective-Sergeant Sussock. Can we get you a drink?'

Big Stevie already had a heavy and a chaser, but he said he'd take a whisky, thank you, sir. This is Glasgow.

'I'll have a lager,' said Sussock to Montgomerie.

'Take a tip and get the bottled lager,' said Big Stevie, pointing to his own glass of heavy. 'It's last night's stuff still in the pipes. It's flat and warm.'

'Bottled lager,' said Sussock, and slid into the seat opposite Big Stevie.

'The only connection I have with Matthew is through GA' said Big Stevie without being prompted by Sussock. 'Has it got him into bother in his work?' Big Stevie lived up to his name. Even seated he was big, broad-shouldered, deep-chested. Sussock recognized another form of bigness about the man, a gentleness of manner, and warm, wise eyes.

'You could say that, Stevie,' said Sussock. 'We think that Matthew has maybe got himself into a mess. We don't know for sure yet, but the indications are not good.'

'Aye,' said Big Stevie in a resigned sort of way. 'I've heard it many times and I'll be hearing it many more times. It's still just as sad. Every time, just as sad.' He looked up and smiled as Montgomerie brought the drinks. They drank each other's health and then Big Stevie said, 'So what do you want to know?'

King and Abernethy sat in the CID rooms writing up.

They were tired, having come in when off duty for the review meeting.

'Catch up on this paperwork while it's quiet,' said King. 'Then back home to get some kip.'

'I could use some,' said Abernethy. 'I could hardly keep my eyes open during the meeting.' He ran his ballpoint over a piece of scrap paper and then, deciding that the pen had run out, consigned it to the waste bin. He took another from his pocket and continued his report.

'Meetings can be like that,' said King.

'I'd like to get home for my dad anyway,' said Abernethy.

'Oh?'

'Yes, we live together, just me and him. He took a stroke a couple of years ago. He'll not recover properly. I don't like to go too long without seeing him.'

'No,' said King. He glanced at Abernethy, very young, fresh-faced, wide-eyed. 'Just you two, is there?'

'Yes. Has been for as long as I can remember.'

'Your dad all right by himself, is he?'

'We have good neighbours and a Home Help three days a week.'

'Good. Well, I dare say this can wait, we'll get off. I'll drop you off at your home. Cambuslang, isn't it?'

'Yes. Thanks. I reckon I'd fall asleep on the bus.' But the 'phone rang. King grabbed it. 'DC King . . . yes . . . Put him on, please . . . yes . . . yes, Tuesday . . .'

Abernethy groaned.

'Yes. I've got it. Stay there. We're on our way.'

'Work?' said Abernethy.

'You'll have to stay awake a little longer.' King stood and reached for his coat. 'That was the fellow Tuesday Noon. Whannell is walking along Garscube Road with a suitcase full of shot-guns.'

CHAPTER 10

Tuesday, October 17, midday

'No, I didn't know he was polis at first,' said Big Stevie, cradling the whisky in his huge fleshy hands which looked as though they had grown soft through unemployment. 'Not at first.'

Sussock asked, 'How long had he been attending Gamblers Anonymous?'

'A few months, about six months.'

'He joined as soon as he came to Glasgow then,' said Montgomerie, more to himself than anyone else.

But Big Stevie picked him up. 'Aye,' he said. 'First time he spoke he told us how gambling had wrecked his life in Edinburgh, ruined his marriage and all, same as many others. He was one for flashy gambling was Matthew, or so he said—you know, casinos and the like. With me it was horses, like most of us in Glasgow, but Matthew went for the glamour as well as the thrill.'

'It is the thrill, isn't it?' said Montgomerie.

'Aye.' Big Stevie didn't disguise his pleasure in finding a sympathetic ear in Montgomerie. 'See that boy over there, studying his form? He's in it for the money, you can tell the serious punters; he'll be happy if he wins, unhappy if he loses. With us, people like me and Matthew and the others, we get hooked on the thrill of not knowing the outcome. Our horse could romp home at a hundred to one, we'd be rich, but we'd put it all on the next race and we couldn't care less if we lost it, because what we want is the excitement of not knowing. You get high on the build-up to the race, and during the race itself. You can feel the adrenalin. But the damage is really great; we build up debts, we raise second mortgages without telling our wives, we take the wife's jewellery piece by piece, bit by bit, pawn it and get some gambling money, we raid our children's piggy banks for fifty pence to put on a nag. Anything for the thrill, and when the race is over all we live for is the next race. It's just a downward spiral and eventually you go to the moneylender, and when they get their claws into you it's the end. A debt for a hundred pounds can become a debt for three hundred within two weeks. There was a moneylender rolled in Maryhill a couple of nights ago; it was the best thing that has happened in a long time.'

'Wee Timmy the Rat?' said Montgomerie. 'I knew him.'

'That's the one, but he's left a gap, there'll be another snake in there in a matter of weeks. Then that's us back to square one, with the moneylenders separating people from their money. You know the latest trick?'

'Tell me,' said Sussock.

'Getting a poor wee wifie, a single parent is the best because they're the most vulnerable, getting her to buy a big item out of a catalogue, say a video recorder for five hundred pounds. They come round and relieve her of it and give her a hundred for her trouble, and sell it in the bars for about four hundred. That's three hundred easy profit for them and the wifie's left to pay off the debt to the catalogue out of her welfare benefit. Nobody will complain; they don't want their heads broken. Gambling drives you into the clutches of people like that.' Big Stevie suddenly got hold of Sussock's hand and held it up to the crown of his head. 'Feel my head,' he said. 'What do you feel?'

'Christ,' said Sussock. He ran his fingers across the top of Big Stevie's head. Amid the hair was a dent in the bone, it felt about an inch wide, maybe quarter of an inch deep.

'I owed a moneylender. The one that ruled Maryhill

before Wee Timmy the Rat. I couldn't pay so he sent his heavies after me, one of them was carrying an axe. The doctor said that I've got one of the thickest skulls he'd ever come across. It saved me, my skull, but it was the end of my working days. I started getting blackouts, can't carry on working as a scaffolder if you take blackouts, no good to yourself, your mates or the people walking on the pavement below you. I had a car too, had to sell it and give up driving. Guess where the money went?'

'The nags,' said Sussock.

'Where else? Now I run this chapter of GA. Gives my life meaning. I haven't had a flutter in two years.'

'Not bad,' said Sussock. 'So tell us about Matthew.'

'Not much to tell, really. He was a member, attended two, three times a week. Spoke, got upset a few days ago but wouldn't tell us anything, stayed for coffee afterwards. Made friends within the group, met up socially, like we all do.'

'Was he friendly with anyone in particular?'

'Aye, he was pally with Hamish Middleton. It was his Post Office which was raided last week. A quarter of a million quid was taken, according to the papers. I reckon Middleton could have done with that money himself.'

'Why do you say that?'

'Well, this is confidential? I mean, it won't go any further.'

'No.'

'Only it would be the end of me and our chapter of GA if it came out how you got this information.'

'We'll keep the source of the information a secret,' said Sussock.

'Well, Middleton, it was him I was thinking of when I said about people taking out second mortgages. He did that about three years ago and didn't want to tell his wife. In the event she disappeared, so that was one less problem for him. He'd also borrowed some money from the sort of unhealthy people we were discussing earlier. He's a frightened man, is Middleton.'

'You don't sound as though you liked him.'

'Liked?'

'Like,' said Sussock quickly. 'It was a slip of the tongue.'

'Oh well, I don't. Bit nose in the air for me, house in Bearsden. It isn't his, isn't his twice over, but he still drives home to his house in lego-land at the end of each working day and lets everyone know it. It surprised me that he and Matthew hit it off, Matthew being a regular guy, a punter's punter.'

'That right?' asked Montgomerie.

'I'm telling you,' said Big Stevie. 'Matthew is all right, always has been with me anyway. I've watched Matthew and Middleton walk away together after a meeting and I've always wondered what they have in common.'

'I wonder?' said Sussock.

'Basically confirms your hypothesis, sir,' said Sussock, standing in front of Donoghue's desk, raincoat hanging open, holding his hat by his side.

Donoghue smiled briefly. 'Confirms it absolutely, I'd say, Ray,' he said. 'Bell and Middleton steeped in debt plan an armed robbery. Middleton provides the method, Bell provides the villains. Subsequently Middleton is bumped off and Bell goes to ground.'

'Certainly looks as though he's gone to ground. Seen jumping into a taxi. Also his handcuffs were used on Middleton.'

'That trace was done, was it?'

'Yes, sir. They were the 'cuffs issued to Bell right enough. I'd say Bell knew he couldn't hide his double role any more and went to join his gang of villains. Wherever they are.'

'How do you think they'll receive him?'

'Open arms I'd say, sir.'

'I don't know, Ray.' Donoghue took his pipe from his mouth and examined the contents of the bowl. 'You see, Ray, villains like to grow their own trees, they like people to serve an apprenticeship, to prove themselves over time. You do not create a gang of hard men and remain their leader just by introducing them to each other. They'll tolerate that so long as they need you, and you'll get away with one job, maybe two. It isn't something you can maintain, especially not if you're a cop. Once a cop, always a cop, as far as a villain is concerned. Middleton didn't last long. We don't know at what point they decided to exclude him from the share-out and until we find Bell we don't know whether he was party to the decision-making.' Donoghue placed his pipe on this desk and sat back in his chair. 'I've been sitting here thinking about Bell's future and I don't think the young man realized what he was creating. It seems such a ruthless outfit that I can't see that Bell would be capable of controlling it. It's a bit like calling up the Devil.'

Sussock breathed deeply. He was silent for a while. Then he said, 'Puts us under a time pressure.'

'Certainly does. Which is why I haven't asked you to take a pew. I've a job for you. King and Abernethy brought in Whannell about half an hour ago, while you were out talking to Big Stevie or whatever you said his name was. I want you to interview Whannell. You know the issues – read over the file first to refresh your memory. We need to know the location of their safe house.'

'But if King and . . .'

'They're both bushed. I've sent them back off duty. Anyway, you know Whannell. Just get on with it, Ray. Like you said, we're under a time pressure.'

As Sussock entered the interview room Constable Piper, who had been standing in the room, left.

'Wait outside,' said Sussock as Piper shut the door. Sussock sat at the table opposite Whannell. Whannell had aged, his face was weatherbeaten, his hair was greasy and matted, the red beard might have been impressive if it had been trimmed.

'Still around, Mr Sussock?' said Whannell, smiling.

'Aye.' Sussock took a packet of cigarettes from his jacket and handed one to Whannell. He took it casually, as though he was sitting with a mate in a saloon bar.

'Aye, they don't get rid of the old soldiers so easy, do they, Ernie?'

'No. We die hard.' Whannell pulled on the cigarette and took the smoke deep into his lungs. 'We go back a long way, you and me, Mr Sussock.'

'Boys of the Old Brigade.' Sussock laid his fag on the round plastic ashtray on which some incarcerated joker had scratched 'This hotel not in guide—poor room service,' and took a pen from his pocket.

'It was you who booked me the very first time. You were a cop in uniform then.'

'I got you time too,' said Sussock. 'With a little help from my friends.'

'Aye,' said Whannell.

'So you're going to cooperate.'

'What else is there to do? I mean, you got me bang to rights, collared red-handed with two unlicensed shotguns—nice guns, gentleman's guns. What do you expect I'd say? It wisnae me?'

'Where did you get the guns from?'

'Off a feller.'

'You can do better than that, Ernie.'

'Aye.'

'Well?'

'I can't tell you.'

'Why?'

'I just can't. Mr Sussock.'

'You've got in with the heavy mob, haven't you?'

'How did you know?'

'We know, Ernie,' said Sussock. 'In fact we know everything. There are just one or two points we'd like to clear up.'

'You mean this is not just about the guns?'

Sussock shook his head. 'You should be so lucky.'

'I don't know what you mean.'

'Don't play dumb, Ernie,' snarled Sussock. 'We're both too old to swallow cat-meat like that. The guns, they're nothing, minor counties south, we're into the big league, the Premier Division. The murder of Flora Middleton two years ago, the Post Office raid last week, the murder of Hamish Middleton.'

'Hamish . . .' Whannell's surprise was obvious, but Sussock didn't allow any leeway.

'Stop playing dumb!'

'Hamish . . . I didn't know.'

'Didn't you? Well, let me tell you, Ernie, he's dead, he's very, very dead and I dare say you had a hand in it.'

'I did not!'

'Just like you had a hand in murdering his wife. It was you that buried her body in the sand dunes near Machrihanish, wasn't it?'

'Yes.' He said it in a soft, clear, deadpan voice, no emotion. 'Yes, I did it, why make a song and dance?'

Sussock was taken aback by the sudden admission. There was a silence which lasted for about ten seconds, but seemed to Sussock to last an hour or more while he searched for words to follow up. But he couldn't get over the ease of getting the confession, he'd been in the room for less than three minutes and there it was, admission to conspiracy to murder. Yes.

'You shot her as well?'

'No.' Whannell shook his head. 'Middleton did that.'

'You were there?'

A nod of the head.

'She was kneeling on the floor,' Sussock began to prompt Whannell. 'He shot her with a twelve-bore.'

'Aye. She was pleading with him. He was drunk, very drunk, he didn't take any notice of her. It was in his home, late one night. You ever heard a shot-gun go off in a small room? I thought it had sent me deaf. I thought all the neighbours would be round, they might have been if he'd shot her again, but as it was nobody came hammering on the door. Middleton dropped the gun and started crying. He told me I had to take her away.'

'Why you?'

'Well, see, Middleton had his claws into me for some money.'

'Not you as well,' said Sussock in a despairing tone.

'Aye. It was big money. Nearly two hundred quid.'

'Two hundred quid,' sniffed Sussock.

'Well, that was big to me, Mr Sussock. Still is.'

'You mean you haven't been paid for the Post Office job yet?'

'No . . . I . . . maybe I shouldn't be telling you this.'

'And maybe you should. Keep talking, Ernie. You're doing just fine.'

'Aye. You know, I feel better just for talking.' Whannell drew on the cigarette. 'So we dumped her body in the car which was in Middleton's garage. There was a door which led from the house to the garage, we didn't have to go outside. Anyway she began moaning, so Middleton hit her on the head with the jack handle. Twice.'

'We'll take a detailed statement about that later, Ernie,' said Sussock. 'What I want now is the information about the boys who did the Post Office job.'

Then Whannell looked worried. He drew on his fag.

'Come on, Ernie.'

Whannell shook his head and dogged the butt.

'Big league frighten you, Ernie?'

'Aye,' he said with escaping breath. 'They're heavy.'

'Not met any like these before?'

Whannell shook his head.

'Frighten you?'

'Aye.'

'How did you get involved?'

'Through Middleton. They wanted a driver at short notice. The one they had lined up was picked up by the Old Bill in Aberdeen on an outstanding warrant.'

'Uh-huh. So Middleton, he . . .'

'He asked me if I could steal a car. If I could he said I'd be part of a job, get a good drink out of it.'

'So you went all the way down to Carlisle to pick up Middleton's old motor. That was a wise move, Ernie.'

'I kept a spare key after Middleton had sold it. I was going to knock it off and sell it. I have this contact in the motor trade who takes bent cars. I knew where his old one was, I'd kept track of it, see. I went down, knocked it off, brought it back and re-sprayed it in a lock-up I have.'

'Where is your lock-up?'

'You'll be wanting to turn it over?'

'Right first time. We'll find items of interest, will we?'

'Televisions and video recorders mostly. I have a contact who can move them. I get them from boys who do people's houses.'

'What then?'

'We drove to meet Middleton's mates. Middleton didn't recognize his old car, not even when he got inside. Jesus, his pals were a heavy duty bunch of hoods. There was no getting out then, not unless I wanted my head blown off. No messing. I was to drive the car on a robbery.'

'It was OK by then, was it? I mean, a wheelman is a trusted position.'

'They didn't want me at first right enough, but

Middleton, he seemed to have some pull and there was this young . . .'

Whannell faltered and glanced at Sussock.

'It's OK, Ernie,' said Sussock. 'We know about DC Bell.'

'Yeah, well, I don't like crooked cops. You're either a cop or a villain. You can't be both.'

'So you pulled the job?'

'Yes. I wasn't told it was Middleton's Post Office that we were to knock over until the day before. It explained Middleton's pull. So that's it.'

'Not quite, Ernie. There were heavy villains, Ernie. Names, please?'

After a pause Whannell said, 'There was a stocky mean guy called Izzy. He was the head man. He had two drogues called Seaweed and Bunny, don't be misled by those names, Mr Sussock, they're both built like a brick shit-house. The others, honestly, I don't know their names. There was also a couple of women. Well, we pulled the job and made the switch and drove off in the delivery van.'

'Straight to the farm?'

'Yes. You know quite a bit.'

'You were seen driving the farm pick-up.'

'Aye, I was sent up to the city to get in the messages. I found the shot-guns in the byre and I thought I'd make a bit by unloading them. Wasn't so easy.'

'Why did you come to Glasgow for the food? Kilmarnock was nearer.'

'Aye, but it's a bit close, Izzy said I had to go into the city where people wouldn't recognize the pick-up. Eventually he stopped me from going, so when he was out one night I just left. I was getting nervous. I didn't care about the money. I took the guns and bedded down in my lock-up.'

'So that's where you were. Why didn't this Izzy want the pick-up noticed?'

'Because the farm is supposed to be empty, Coles Copse Farm is.'

'Coles Copse Farm, is it, Ernie?'

Whannell was silent for a while and then said, 'I would have told you if you'd asked me, Mr Sussock.'

'Aye,' said Sussock.

'Empty, sir,' said the detective-sergeant of the Kilmarnock Police. About thirty-five, Donoghue guessed, quite relaxed and confident, secure in his role. Sussock stood next to Donoghue, Montgomerie stood behind Sussock.

'Completely empty?' Donoghue raised his eyebrows and then consulted the Hunter which he kept in his waistcoat pocket, secured by a gold chain.

'Yes, sir. Except for the corpse of course.'

'Of course.' Donoghue slipped the watch back into the pocket.

'We thought we'd not take the body away until you had inspected the locus of the crime.'

'Very thoughtful of you, Sergeant. But the rest of the house is empty?'

'Yes, sir. We came straight up here as soon as we received your call, but by the time we arrived, the place had been empty for some hours, a full day perhaps, going on the remains of the fire in the grate. We have searched from rafters to cellar. Nothing.'

'I see.'

'They even burnt their garbage before leaving, a professional touch if there ever was one.'

'They were professional men.'

'We're dusting for prints now, but I don't think we've turned anything up.'

'I don't think you ever will,' said Donoghue.

*

Coles Copse farm house was a squat and rambling building. It had faded whitewashed walls and a roof of dull grey slate which had sagged in places. At the side of the building was a byre, a tall structure of rotting timber, which Donoghue fancied would probably collapse during the first gale of the coming winter. At the front of the house were three police cars and a dark blue mortuary van.

'Well,' said Donoghue, 'shall we go in? Lead on, please, Sergeant.'

The main downstairs room of the farmhouse was long and narrow. Old armchairs squatted on the flagstone floor. The black and grey embers of a wood fire lay behind an iron grate. To Donoghue, Sussock and Montgomerie, Matthew 'Ding-Dong' Bell looked the same as always. Except that for the first time he was seen prostrate, his eyes were open and there was a small hole in his skull, just above his left ear.

An adolescent-looking man stood with the fingers of his hands interlocked in front of his chest in a prayer-like gesture and held his head slightly bowed. A black bag stood at his feet.

'Dr Fishlock, our surgeon,' said the detective-sergeant by way of introduction. 'DI Donoghue, from Glasgow.'

Donoghue and the frail young man shook hands. Donoghue thought: My God, they're getting young, so young. Then he asked, 'Have you been able to establish a cause of death, sir?'

'Not without a full post-mortem, Mr Donoghue, but I'm fairly certain it will turn out to be the gunshot wound you can see there. There is no exit wound, so I should be able to give you the bullet for your ballistics people to work on.'

'No exit wound?' repeated Donoghue.

'None, and a small entry wound. I'd say it will turn out

to be a bullet from a .22 calibre gun. Very lethal weapons if you know where to aim them.'

'Such as just above the ear.'

'Exactly,' said Dr Fishlock. 'This particular round seems to have been fired from a distance of, oh, greater than two to three feet; you'll notice the hair hasn't been singed by the blast. I'll be able to say more when I find out how far the bullet has penetrated. I'll be sending a full report as soon as I've done the PM. May I take the body away now?'

'Yes, yes, of course,' said Donoghue quietly.

Montgomerie said, 'I wish to God his eyes would close.'

In Donoghue's Rover, it was Montgomerie, sitting in the rear seat, who against all protocol broke the silence. He said simply, 'He was a victim.'

'What!' said Sussock from the front passenger seat.

'Ding-Dong was,' Montgomerie repeated. 'I've been thinking that we have to be big-minded. He wasn't a bent cop, not Ding-Dong, he was a victim.'

Donoghue changed gear for no apparent reason and pressed the accelerator to the floor.

'Just another victim,' said Montgomerie as he felt the seat press into the small of his back.